Puffin Books

HOW TO SURVIVE

If you go hiking, camping, climbing or canoeing – or if you ever travel by land, sea or air – you have probably wondered what it would be like to be lost or stranded in an unfamiliar part of the world, perhaps even a different country, with no one to help you and very little equipment to use. It would be difficult to survive, but if you've read this book your chances would be much greater.

It is a book about how to overcome hazards. It tells you how to prepare your own personal pocket survival kit in a tobacco tin; how to build a shelter to keep you warm and dry; how to build fires and light them without matches; how to trap animals for food; how to test plants for edibility; how to find water in dry regions; the safest way of travelling and what to do when you are lost. It includes all the international call codes and signals. It teaches you how to use a map and a compass and, if you are lost without either, how to tell your direction from the sun and stars. It even tells you how to make all sorts of useful things from natural materials – from bivouacs to rafts and from ovens to sandals and snowshoes. Robinson Crusoe would have found life much easier had he read *How to Survive*.

Brian Hildreth has many years' experience of teaching survival techniques. He is the author of the *New Zealand Air Force Survival Handbook*, which has sold many thousands of copies, and he has written this book specially for young people.

The greatest aids to survival are good common sense backed up by some knowledge of the problems you face and how to overcome them. *How to Survive* will probably be the most practical and valuable book you will ever read.

HOW TO SURVIVE

Written by Brian Hildreth
Illustrated by Conrad Bailey

Puffin Books

Puffin Books, Penguin Books Ltd, Harmondsworth, Middlesex, England
Penguin Books, 625 Madison Avenue, New York, New York 10022, U.S.A.
Penguin Books Australia Ltd, Ringwood, Victoria, Australia
Penguin Books Canada Ltd, 2801 John Street, Markham, Ontario, Canada L3R 1B4
Penguin Books (N.Z.) Ltd, 182–190 Wairau Road, Auckland 10, New Zealand

First published by Puffin Books 1976
Reprinted 1976, 1978, 1980, 1982

Text copyright © Brian Hildreth, 1976
Illustrations copyright © Conrad Bailey, 1976
All rights reserved

Made and printed in Great Britain by
Richard Clay (The Chaucer Press) Ltd
Bungay, Suffolk
Set in Monotype Ehrhardt

Contents

1. Survival Knowledge

If you ever travel by air; make a sea voyage; go hiking, hunting, camping, canoeing, climbing; get stranded in a snowstorm, earthquake or forest fire – you may suddenly be faced with the necessity to **survive**, perhaps in a part of the world you do not know at all.

This book is a 'do-it-yourself' manual for survivors, and no matter where you may be, it will help you to cope with emergency situations in the outdoors when your **survival** is entirely dependent on your own efforts.

PREPARATION

The change from a normal, everyday existence to a *surviva situation* is generally very sudden, and almost invariably you don't have a great deal of time to think about it.

Modern living, because of all the amenities it provides, does not teach us to be very good at surviving on our own. Our reactions have become dulled and sluggish because we no longer need to rely on them for our survival. We have become so accustomed to pressing a switch when we want power or light, turning on a tap when we want water, and visiting a store when we want tools or clothes or food, that we tend to forget the hazards Nature can produce. In fact, they seem so remote from our lives that they appear to have been eliminated altogether. But these hazards do exist, and in a survival situation you can be brought face to face with them very rapidly.

It is the person with survival knowledge who is best equipped to overcome many of the unpleasant effects which sudden disaster in the outdoors may produce.

You may think your situation is hopeless, but by studying the information in this book, by applying the techniques it suggests, and by practising as many of them as possible before you need them, there will never be any necessity for you to feel helpless, or to despair, no matter what situation you may find yourself in.

PREPARATION FOR SURVIVAL

Being in a survival situation, where staying alive despite all dangers is your major concern, is almost always without exception – tough, unpleasant and uncomfortable – and there is no sense in pretending it isn't.

If you have the determination to survive, together with a knowledge of the mental problems involved in survival, you can accomplish far more than may have ever seemed possible.

FEAR

. . . but thy hands are loosed and weak
and the blood has left thy cheek
it is Fear O little Hunter, it is Fear.
          – *Rudyard Kipling*

Fear is a perfectly normal reaction when you are faced with dangerous circumstances. In fact, to be completely fearless would lessen your chances of survival because you would be liable to make disastrous mistakes. But there is a difference in experiencing fear, and giving way to irrational fear in the way that Kipling's 'little Hunter' did. He plunged his spear 'in the empty mocking thicket', and it is these empty mocking thickets of your own imagination which you need to understand when you are 'thinking through' your mental preparation for survival.

It is helpful to classify fear under various headings, because by doing this you may at least recognize the various forms, and by positive action place them firmly under control.

There are three main fears faced by most survivors of disasters and together they may add up to such a state of apprehension and terror that they become the greatest hazard to be faced. These fears are:

> Fear of the unknown
> Fear of your own weakness
> Fear of discomfort

Fear of the unknown is always a product of your imagination, and while a lively imagination is no bad thing under normal circumstances, it can play havoc with you under conditions of stress. It's no comfort to be told in a book like this that it is only your imagination which sees a tiger lurking behind every tree – what you really want is a way to rid yourself of the fear, or at least take your mind off it.

Fortunately there is such a way, and it is based on a most important principle of survival – **Action!** No matter what situation you find yourself in, there is always something you can do to overcome difficulties. Every survival situation is different, but the principles to be applied for successful survival are universal, and they all start with one important requirement – **a plan of action**.

Knowledge is the key and by studying the material in this book you have taken the first step towards dispelling fear of the unknown.

Fear of your own weakness is simply another way of saying,

'I lack confidence in my knowledge and ability.' If you have had outdoor experience, this fear is not likely to affect you as much as it will someone who has had little or no experience. If you fall into the latter category, then practising some, or all, of the skills mentioned in this book will help to overcome this. Even if this is not possible, there is no reason for you to despair. Tell yourself, and keep on telling yourself, '**I will succeed. Others have done it and so will I!**'

Fear of discomfort is a very real and gnawing fear, which is not only due to having no adequate shelter or a comfortable bed. It is also due to loneliness.

The physical aspects of discomfort can be overcome much more easily than loneliness, and once again study of techniques described in this book for making shelters, fires, beds and equipment, together with methods of finding and preparing food, can do a great deal to remove excessive discomfort. Mental discomfort in the form of loneliness is not so easy to deal with, but applying your **plan of action** can help a great deal. If you are concentrating on staying alive, and actively doing something about getting yourself back into the world of men, then the periods when you feel lonely will be considerably reduced.

WILL TO LIVE

There are countless stories of survivors who lived despite doing all the 'wrong things', and in some cases even went beyond the point where medical science would declare they should be dead.

If you investigate these extreme cases one factor invariably appears – an indomitable *will to live*. You can enlist this same sense of self-preservation yourself. When the odds facing you seem almost insuperable, your will to live, and an equally strong determination never to stop trying, can carry you through. **Tell yourself, and keep on telling yourself** you will succeed – and you will! To be a survivor you must never stop trying – never!

FORMULA FOR SURVIVAL

None of the information in this book is of the slightest use to you if you can't remember it. And the time when you are most likely to need the information is when it is even more difficult to recall – when you are in a survival situation.

I have devised a five-word sentence to help you to overcome this difficulty. It is easy to remember, and the initial letters of the words in this sentence are the initial letters of the five important requirements for survival.

> '*Priority First Actions When Foundered*'
>
> 'P' – *P*rotection against the environment
> 'F' – *F*irst Aid
> 'A' – *A*ids
> 'W' – *W*ater
> 'F' – *F*ood

You will notice that the sentence itself says 'this is what you must concentrate on above everything else', and then provides you with the pegs to hang your actions and requirements on. So there you have it – the survival formula!

Prepare yourself for survival now – learn the sentence and repeat it to yourself at regular intervals until it is engraved in your mind. Some day, somewhere, it could help save your life.

Throughout the book each of the five important requirements for survival are dealt with, so once you have thoroughly learnt the sentence you can use it as a mental filing system to organize your survival knowledge into a definite plan.

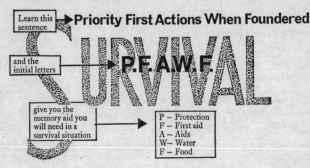

Fig. 1 The survival formula

A PERSONAL POCKET SURVIVAL KIT

There is a party game which is a great test of ingenuity, in which you try to put as many complete and recognizable articles into a matchbox as you can. The preparation of a personal pocket survival kit is rather like this competition, although the container used should be a little larger than a matchbox – a standard-size tobacco tin (11 cm × 8 cm × 2 cm deep) is ideal. You can put a variety of things into the tin, all of which will play a vital role in a survival situation. Carry it with you always.

The really important consideration when making such a kit, or any survival equipment at all, is to ensure that nothing superfluous is carried and that everything serves a useful purpose. The kit described here follows this rule. Every part of it – including the container itself – is a useful survival aid.

If you are often in the outdoors, or travel a great deal, you will find that because this kit occupies so little space and weighs only about 120 grams, it is extremely easy to have with you always. Even carried in the glove-box of a car it provides a comprehensive and useful 'tool'. (Don't forget to replace any item you may use from it.)

This list is made up of things I personally have found extremely useful, but there is no reason for you to stick religiously to it as long as nothing really important (like matches) is left out. You can make it as individual as you wish.

1. The *Container* itself: a tobacco tin is excellent because it is easily slipped into your pocket; it is strong and simple to keep waterproof; it can be used as a small cooking utensil; and it makes an excellent heliograph signalling device (see page 18).
2. *Matches and Striker*   As these are two of the most important survival aids you can have, they are top priority in your kit. It is well worth taking a little extra time to waterproof the matches. All you need to do is to melt some candle wax in a small container and dip each match-head into the wax (or drip melted wax from a candle on to the heads). Put the waxed matches into a small plastic bag, wrap them tightly and seal the parcel by binding it with sticking plaster or electrical insulation tape. Cut the striker from the side of a matchbox and seal it in plastic in the same way. Then both matches and striker can be fastened together to make one small bundle. Make a really thorough job of the waterproofing and sealing, so that even if your kit is immersed in water for a considerable period the matches and striker will remain dry and usable until they are unwrapped.
3. *Candle*   This is not for providing light, but for lighting a fire under difficult conditions. A piece of candle about 5 cm in length is suitable, or, alternatively, a few of the thin birthday candles used for cake decoration. As firelighters, candles are unbeatable, and with skill it is possible to 'feed' one with small sticks until a small fire is started, and to retrieve the candle before it is consumed.

4. *Whistle* A small whistle, with a shrill and penetrating note, is a useful signalling device to include in your kit. You can generally buy one for a few pence. Tie a loop of string to the whistle so that you can hang it round your neck.

5. *Compass* A small, cheap magnetic compass should be included, but remember that the metal container will affect it to some extent, and you won't be able to perform precise navigational work with it. It will be inaccurate after it has been sealed up for some time, but it will still give you a rough idea where north is.

6. *Razor Blade* The best type to include in the kit has only one cutting edge, and a strengthening piece of metal along the other edge. It is easy to handle, and does not break as readily as the two-edged variety. You can include a small pocket knife instead of the razor blade, but make sure it is very sharp.

7. *String* A hank of strong string at least 3 metres in length. Make sure you test it to ensure that it doesn't break easily when under strain. (A point to remember – your boot- or shoelaces are 'cord' and can sometimes be used to increase the length of a piece of string used for fishing or making a snare. Don't forget to retrieve your shoelaces after they have been used, though.)

8. *Needle and Thread* A stout needle (5 cm long) threaded through a small piece of cardboard and then wound with about 5 metres of very strong thread all wrapped in a piece of thin plastic does not take up much room. The needle can be used for removing thorns and splinters, and complete with its cotton can be used for repairing tears in clothing.

9. *Fishing Line (Trace) and Hooks* Several metres of nylon trace with a breaking strain of about 4–5 kg, together with 3 or 4 hooks of various sizes. It pays to protect the ends of the hooks with small pieces of cork

to save them from penetrating yourself or any of the equipment in your kit.

10. *Safety Pins*   At least two about 5 cm long. Excellent for quick repairs to clothing, and for fastening bandages or dressings. You can pin them on the cardboard with the needle.

11. *Rubber Tubing*   This apparently surprising item in your kit (recommended size: 5 mm outside diameter, length 60 cm) can be used as a 'spring' for a trap for small animals; and is extremely useful for obtaining drinking water from difficult or inaccessible places, such as small depressions in fallen logs, or among rocks.

12. *First-Aid Materials*   A few *sticking-plaster dressings* (the type which are sterile until removed from their wrapper), a *roller bandage* (3 cm wide), and a *small roll of plain sticking plaster*, and *plain gauze pad* (about 15 cm × 90 cm). (It seems large, but if a piece of gauze this size is folded to fit the bottom of the container it will go in easily.)

13. *Condys Crystals in a Plastic Bag*   This item is included for use as an *antiseptic*, a *water purifier*, a *firelighter* and a *snow marker*. You need only a small quantity of the Condys Crystals for first aid (only a few grains), about ½ a teaspoon for fire-lighting and as much as you can fit into the kit for snow marking. You can buy your Condys Crystals (chemical name – *potassium permanganate* or *permanganate of potash*) from a chemist, and include about one large teaspoonful in your kit, *sealed securely* in a small plastic bag. This chemical is easily soluble in water and produces a beautiful deep red.

14. *Sugar*   If you decide you would like to carry a 'back-up' fire-lighting method other than matches, then include a few teaspoonfuls of sugar in a plastic bag. (You need Condys Crystals for this method, so if you don't have them in your kit, don't worry about the sugar.)

USING YOUR CONDYS CRYSTALS:

First Aid	A few grains dissolved in clean water produce an excellent **antiseptic solution** for washing away dirt from around wounds. The survival-kit container makes a good 'bowl' for preparing the solution.
Water Purifying	A few grains added to one litre of water, which is then allowed to stand for 30 minutes or longer, purifies quite efficiently – the faint red colour in the purified water is not harmful. This treatment should be applied to all non-flowing water before drinking.
Fire-lighting	This is an emergency use to which you can apply your **Condys Crystals**, provided you also have some sugar. (The method is described under **fire-lighting** on page 51.)
Snow Marker	Sprinkled on snow, and, if necessary, stirred around a little, Condys Crystals make a very effective signal marker.

15. *Nails* Two 10-cm nails are a useful addition to your kit, and although not absolutely essential can be put to a variety of uses, such as making a *fish spear* (see page 128), preparing a deadfall trap (see page 124), or, in their more useful role, joining pieces of wood together.

16. *A Piece of Notepaper* It is no problem to include this, and it is much easier to leave or send a written message on a piece of paper than to try and find something suitable to write on. It can also be used as tinder for lighting a fire – a **signal fire** in particular (see page 78).

17. *Pencil* You need only a short piece of pencil (5–6 cm long), and if you are also going to use your survival kit

container as a **heliograph** (see p. 18), then the pencil should be fastened to it by a short piece of string, securely knotted through a hole at top-centre, in the front of the tin (see Fig. 2).

When your kit is finally assembled and carefully packed it should be sealed right round with electrical insulation tape, or other waterproof tape. Then seal the kit inside a plastic bag to ensure that it is completely waterproof. (The bag also becomes a useful aid.)

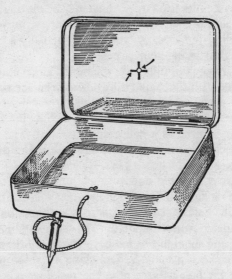

Fig. 2 Heliograph and pocket survival kit

Make yourself a personal survival kit and acquire the habit of carrying it with you whenever you go on an outdoor expedition – no matter how short or long it may be. It is a great comfort to know you are always prepared for an emergency.

HOW TO MAKE AND USE A HELIOGRAPH

A heliograph is a signalling device which uses the light from the sun to send a strong flashing signal to a target such as a searching aeroplane, boat or search party which may be a long way off. The difficulty with flashing signals is ensuring that they actually 'hit the target'. If you have ever had someone shine the light from a mirror in your eyes you will know how effective such a signal can be, but to direct light over several miles to a target which may be moving requires a little more preparation than just shining a mirror in its general direction, because you cannot actually see the reflected light striking your target.

To overcome this difficulty, you need a target close to you and in line with the main target – perhaps an aeroplane, or a boat. A pencil, tied to the front of the personal-survival-kit container (which must have a lid with a shiny inner surface if it is to be used as a heliograph), is ideal. The distance from the container to where the string is tied to the pencil should be approximately 15 cm.

All that is required now is a hole punched through the centre of the lid. This can be done when you first make the kit, and the hole sealed with a piece of sticking plaster, or it can be made when required. The hole is for sighting through, and shouldn't be too big – about half the diameter of a match stick is enough. Scratching a 'cross' inside the lid, with the hole as its centre, can make your heliograph a little more precise in action, but it isn't absolutely essential.

USING THE HELIOGRAPH

The diagram shows you how the heliograph should be held when you want to send a signal.

These are the points to remember:

1. A heliograph only works when the sun is shining!
2. It does make a very distinctive signal which may be seen a long way off – even by the pilot or observers in an aeroplane flying at several thousand feet.
3. You don't need to have the sun directly in front of you to make the signal – you simply turn the reflecting lid at an

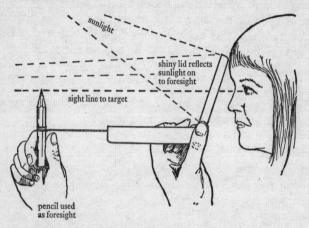

Fig. 3 Signalling with a heliograph

angle until it catches the sunlight and then you can direct it where you want it to go.
4. It is not necessary to try and make the signal 'flash'. The slight vibrations of your hands do the job for you.
5. It pays to practise using your heliograph so you will know exactly how to use it effectively.

Having decided where you wish to direct the signal, hold the pencil upright, as shown, with the string stretched tight.

Sight through the hole in the lid, and line up the tip of the pencil with the target. Now move the lid of the container, turning it towards the sun until you are able to reflect the sunlight on to your hand. (The hole through the lid will actually make a dark spot which you may be able to see on your hand or fingers.) Check you are still on target with the tip of the pencil, then move the lid until the reflected sunlight shines on the tip of the pencil and hold steady. A beam of light will now be directed at the target.

The **personal survival kit** and heliograph have been described in some detail because I cannot overstate the importance of having such **survival aids**. The survival information in this book, however, assumes that you will have very little equipment – or no equipment at all.

P – F – A – W – F

Go back to page 12 now and check that the **survival formula** is firmly fixed in your mind!

2. Survival First Aid

Survival first aid is first aid of a very special, and fairly limited, kind. Its most important characteristic is that it is easily remembered without any complicated rules.

Survivors of disasters of any kind are often shocked and confused, and in such a condition it is difficult to recall complex procedures, or even to remember that there are any procedures at all! What is required, and what is given here, is a first-aid formula which can be engraved in your mind so that under survival conditions you will instinctively recall the life-saving first-aid principles you need.

EIGHT IMPORTANT WORDS

The first-aid formula to be committed to memory consists of eight words, and these eight words are composed of four pairs; so this is how you should memorize them – in pairs.

> 1. Stop bleeding
> 2. Protect wound
> 3. Immobilize fractures
> 4. Treat shock

These eight words are the essentials of self-administered survival first aid, and they are the key which opens your personal first-aid filing cabinet of information.

Learn these eight words in their pairs now! Repeat them to yourself as often as possible until you can recall them without a moment's hesitation.

STOP BLEEDING

Your blood is your life, and regardless of all other conditions, such as fractures, **bleeding must be stopped,** promptly, by any means available.

There are three main types of bleeding:

1. **Arterial** – this type is present when an artery is cut or torn. The blood is bright red and spurts out in time with each heart beat.
Arterial bleeding must be stopped quickly.
2. **Venous** – the blood is dark red and flows steadily.
3. **Capillary** – blood oozes out.

To stop bleeding – act quickly

1. If blood is spurting, **press with fingers directly into wound,** regardless of blood.
2. If you can make a pad from a handkerchief or bit of clothing without wasting time – apply to wound, and maintain pressure until bleeding slows and a pressure bandage can be applied. (If you have no bandage, a pressure pad made from a folded piece of cloth may be held in place on the wound with the sleeve or tail of a shirt, a belt or the long, fibrous leaf of a plant.)
3. If a wound bleeds copiously before you are able to stop the bleeding –
   – Do not attempt to wash wound.
   – Do not remove any clotted blood.
   Doing either of these things may start the bleeding again.
   Your blood is your life – stop bleeding – at once.

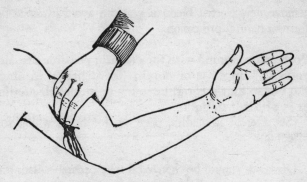

If blood is spurting press fingers directly into wound.
BUT— do not do this if there is any broken glass or
jagged metal in the wound.

Fig. 4 Stop bleeding – QUICKLY

PROTECT WOUND

Under survival conditions it is doubly important that you
make every effort to protect wounds of any size from being
infected. Protection of a wound against further damage is
also important, as well as lessening discomfort, since knock-
ing an exposed wound can be extremely painful.

Protecting a wound to prevent infection and further
damage also includes cleaning the wound, if it is at all possible. If you can wash it with water before covering it with
a dressing improvised from a clean handkerchief or piece of
clothing (if you lack a first-aid kit), do so, *provided* the
water is fresh and obviously not polluted. Normally, if a
first-aid kit is available, you would try and cleanse the
wound with an **antiseptic solution**, such as the weak
Condys solution you could make if you had a personal
survival kit. If no antiseptic is available, but you are able to
heat water, then water which has been boiled and then
cooled should be used. When cleaning a wound do not

remove dry, clotted blood if you can avoid it, since this forms a natural protection.

Protect any wound with the cleanest possible dressing you can improvise or obtain. Tie it firmly in place, but not so that it is tight enough to hinder circulation or is difficult to undo.

(See Herbal Remedies, page 33, for herbs which stop bleeding.)

Dressings should be changed if they become soiled, provided you have sufficient materials – otherwise leave the dressing undisturbed.

Burns – these are wounds which also need protecting, both from the air and from further contamination. Small burns should be covered with a dressing of clean cloth and left alone. Large burns are easily infected and should not be touched, since they are sterile from the heat which caused the burn. Cover with several layers of cloth, such as strips of shirt or other clothing, and try to avoid exposing the area for any longer than necessary.

IMMOBILIZE FRACTURES

To be a survivor with a fractured limb is serious, but not hopeless. 'Immobilize' means 'prevent from moving', and as a solo survivor the only possible treatment is for you to try and immobilize the broken bone to prevent movement of the broken ends. **This immobilization of a break is vital, since if it is not done further damage may result, and shock will be increased.**

Broken Upper Limb

A broken upper limb should be fastened against the body, if possible, and cradled in a fold of clothing to give it support. A self-applied splint is difficult, but not impossible, but utilizing the body itself as a splint is the best way to hold an upper limb immobile.

Fig. 5 Sling formed from clothing

Fractured Leg or Ankle

A fractured leg or ankle puts you in a difficult survival situation – you have to survive where you are – any possibility of moving more than a few metres is very doubtful.

If a leg is fractured below the knee, you have two possible courses of action – you can try splinting it with pieces of padded sticks tied firmly in place above and below the fracture; or you can tie the fractured leg to the uninjured leg using strips of clothing.

A fractured thighbone is much more difficult to immobilize than a lower limb – but you must make every effort to do so, and to move as little as possible.

Raising a broken limb will help to relieve swelling and pain. Lying on the ground, for example, you may be able to lift the injured leg on to a log or boulder.

People have survived in the wilds with broken legs and have been rescued.

Never give up hope.

If you can possibly light a fire, you should do so. It will help to combat shock; will keep you warm; and provides an important guide for rescuers.

TREAT SHOCK

Shock is a serious condition which can cause death, and it must be considered present and be treated whenever you are injured – even if you do not think you are suffering from its effects.

If you suffer from the effects of shock, your survival chances are considerably reduced, and in its extreme form complete collapse of the nervous system controlling your heart, breathing and blood circulation may occur.

A solo survivor from any disaster, whether injured or not, must assume that shock will be present at some time – it doesn't always appear immediately: there may be several hours' delay before it takes effect.

You are Your Own Doctor

Most books on first aid give advice on the procedure you should follow if treating someone for shock, and invariably the advice starts or finishes with 'keep the patient warm and get a doctor'. Under 'normal' circumstances this is excellent advice, but things are completely different when you are on your own and a doctor is not available – you must be your own doctor – and to treat shock this is what you must do:

1. Protect yourself from the effects of wind, rain, cold or excessive heat by immediately getting into the best shelter you can find. (See Shelter, page 60.)

2. As soon as you find adequate shelter, sit down and attend to any injuries.
3. With injuries cared for, lie down and make yourself as comfortable and warm as you possibly can. Tight clothing should be loosened, and your feet raised about a hand's breadth on to an object that will support them.
4. Rest in your sheltered position until you feel strong enough to carry on. This may require several hours, or even complete inactivity for a day or more, but **unless you ensure that shock has been treated your efficiency will remain so low that you won't be able to carry on anyway.**
5. Drink plenty of water, or a hot, sweet drink (if you are lucky enough to have something to make it with) as soon as you are able to.

If you are the victim of a disaster, shock can, and often does occur even when no injuries are present. If injuries are present, shock is unavoidable.

Whether **injured** or **uninjured**, as the survivor of any kind of disaster you must assume that shock will affect you.

Other Injuries

Sprains commonly occur at the wrist or ankle, and are the result of stretched or torn ligaments round a joint. They are painful but not always serious, and there is always swelling round the affected joint.

The best treatment is to apply a *cold* wet cloth to the sprain and, if possible, raise the joint.

A sprained wrist should be supported in a sling close to the body, and a sprained ankle should be firmly bandaged with a strip of cloth in a figure-of-eight (pass bandage under the foot, across over the instep, cross again behind ankle, then bring to front and tie). If the joint swells, remove the bandage, soak it in cold water, and re-apply.

If you have to move a considerable distance with a sprained ankle, fasten a figure-of-eight bandage over the *outside* of your boot or shoe; rest the joint frequently, and raise it each time you stop.

THINGS TO GUARD AGAINST

FROST-BITE

Frost-bite is a serious injury which must be guarded against at all costs. **Prevention** is the best line of defence against frost-bite, because once you have it, it is impossible to get rid of it.

Frost-bite occurs at sub-zero temperatures, and the symptoms are sometimes not recognized until too late. You may feel a prickling sensation, but this is not always the case. Patches of white, wax-like, numb skin, which is stiff and firm to the touch, may appear, and if frost-bite is **not treated at this stage the skin may freeze, leading to blistering and death of the affected part**, following extreme pain and swelling.

Prevention: Keep as warm and dry as possible, and protect all exposed skin. If you have no mittens, socks worn on hands offer some protection. Crumple up your toes in your boots or shoes at regular intervals, and pull faces to exercise your face muscles. Feel for stiffening spots on skin continuously.

If symptoms appear **do not attempt to rub the affected area**. The best treatment is **human warmth** from breath or warm hands. Tepid to warm water may also be used, but in your situation it will probably be difficult to apply this kind of treatment. Frost-bitten fingers may be warmed in your armpits.

Never rub frost-bite with snow or try to thaw by a fire – doing either of these things will make the condition worse.

SNOW-BLINDNESS AND GLARE-BLINDNESS

Snow-blindness is an extremely painful injury to the eyes caused by reflection of sunlight – and in particular the ultra-violet rays in the sunlight – from snow.

Glare-blindness is caused by the reflection of the sun and its damaging rays from water or large expanses of sand.

To be a survivor is a difficult enough situation without being a blind survivor – snow-blindness or glare-blindness must be prevented at all costs.

Prevention: You must cut down the amount of light striking the eyes but at the same time retain your ability to see where you are going. There are several ways to do this, and waste no time if you are being subjected to glare.

1. If you are wearing a hat, pull the brim down over the eyes as far as possible. (This does not offer complete protection, but does reduce direct sunlight.)
2. **Blacken** upper cheeks and around the eyes with any black material – **mud, soot, charcoal.** This will reduce reflection.
3. **Cover** eyes with improvised 'goggles'. The Eskimoes, who appreciate the danger of snow-blindness, make protective goggles from wood or bone with a fine slit cut through it for vision. You can make the same kind of goggles from cardboard, paper, leather or a plastic belt – in fact anything which is easily cut – and then fasten it in place round the face. Make cross-shaped slits for the best visibility.

The effort involved is worth it!

4. **Plant material** of a fibrous nature, such as grass or leaves shredded into strips, can be tied in place over the eyes and still allow enough vision to enable free movement. The diagram shows how the band which holds the face-screen can also secure a piece of cloth to protect the top of your head as well as the back of your neck and ears.
5. **Cloth** with an open weave (some handkerchiefs have such a texture) can be tied round the forehead so that a large flap hangs down over the eyes and face. If the cloth is big enough to reach under the chin, it should be tucked into clothing round the neck and, if possible, should

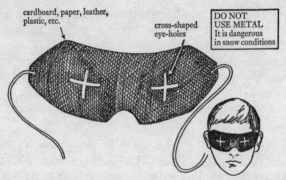

cardboard, paper, leather, plastic, etc.

cross-shaped eye-holes

DO NOT USE METAL
It is dangerous in snow conditions

Fig. 6 Improvised goggles for protection against snow-blindness and glare

cover the ears too, since ultra-violet rays are reflected upwards from a reflecting surface, and areas which do not normally receive much sunlight can be severely burnt.

Treatment if you are Caught

If snow-blindness or glare-blindness should attack you unawares, you won't be in any doubt about the condition. Your eyes will water and turn red, and will feel as though they contain hot sand. (These symptoms may take twelve to twenty-four hours to appear.) If the burning is acute, your eyes will water profusely, pus will form and the eyelids will stick together.

To treat snow- or glare-blindness, apply cold cloths to the eyes and leave them in position until they become warm, then change them. **Cloths can be chilled by application of snow, by placing on ice or by soaking in cold water.**

Continue this treatment for at least thirty minutes, and

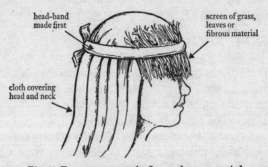

head-band made first

screen of grass, leaves or fibrous material

cloth covering head and neck

Fig. 7 Face-screen made from plant material

repeat three times a day. Pouring a stream of cool water into the eyes several times a day is also soothing.

Your eyes are an extremely important survival 'tool' – Protect them no matter how inconvenient it may seem!

SNOWBURN AND SUNBURN

Snowburn and sunburn are both caused by over-exposure of the skin to the burning ultra-violet light present in sunlight.

Prevention is not always easy, but, like any burn, snowburn and sunburn are serious conditions and

your survival chances are limited if you should be badly affected.

Resist the temptation to remove clothing in the hot sun – **keep as much bare skin covered as possible**, and take particular care that the back of your neck is protected.

If you get burned **treatment** is difficult, but apply cold, wet cloths to soothe the burns, and drink lots of water.

HERBAL REMEDIES

The herbs listed below beside the ailments they relieve, are all proven remedies. No diagrams of these plants are given, however, owing to the very great difficulty of accurate identification of plants from diagrams.

If you are not sure of your identification of these plants, it is better not to use them. No plant in the list is poisonous, but it is very easy to identify wrongly plants with similar leaf shapes. Always remember the plant you gather might be harmful.

Use and apply these herbs with confidence if you know them; otherwise, don't try. Being a survivor is bad enough without making your situation worse!

(Advance your survival training another step by learning to identify these plants correctly before you need them. Consult an expert – you'll find that most people who know herbs are generally delighted to talk about them.)

Note: Many of the plants listed in the table below will not be found growing wild, but old mining camps, deserted huts and cottages, are often found to have had gardens in which some of these plants have persisted.

Ailment	Herb	How to apply
Insect stings and Stinging nettle	Scarlet Pimpernel	Crush leaf and spit on it before applying directly
	Plantain	Apply a freshly cut slice
	Onion (wild or cultivated)	Apply a freshly cut slice
Bee stings	Golden Rod	Grind flowers into a pulp
Sunburn and Burns generally	Witch Hazel Yarrow	Steep flowers in water for a soothing lotion
	Elder Tree	Steep leaves, flowers or berries for a lotion
Bleeding (if bleeding is severe, apply direct pressure. See page 22)	Yarrow, Periwinkle, Bistort, Knapweed, Horse-tail, Shepherd's Purse, Lady's Mantle, Golden Rod	Crush the leaves of any of these plants and apply directly to the cut
	Herb Robert	Use the root of this herb
Bruises and Sprains	Golden Rod, Scabious (or Devil's Bit), Marigold, Sweet Cicely, Archangel (Yellow and White)	Apply a cold compress by bruising leaves of any of these plants and binding in place with a bandage, piece of cloth from clothing or long, fibrous leaf
Toothache	Yarrow	Chew the leaves

Can you recall the eight-word first-aid formula?
Turn back to page 21 and check your memory!

3. Exposure

Overcoming hazards is what **survival** is all about. The hazards you face may be many and varied, and how you deal with them determines whether you will come through your survival experience in good shape – but there is one hazard over which you have no direct control – the **climate**. And climate has a great deal to do with another condition which must be guarded against.

Exposure is a very nasty condition which happens when warmth is removed from the body by continuous chilling. The weather conditions which can bring about this chilling consist of a combination of:

> 1. Cold
> 2. Moisture (rain, sleet, melted snow, fog and some-times sweat)
> 3. Wind

Any of these three factors – **cold/wet/wind** – may be uncomfortable, but combined they are at their deadliest.

YOU ARE A WARM-BLOODED ANIMAL

Your normal body temperature remains constantly around 37° Celsius, even though the temperature of the environment you are in may be higher (a hot climate), or lower (a warm, moderate or cool climate). Your body maintains its constant temperature by various means, such as sweating when too hot, and shivering (which generates heat) when too cold, and by such means the **heat lost** from the body is balanced against **heat produced**. Since you are a warm-blooded member of the animal kingdom, you are your own 'heat factory' – reptiles can bask in the sun and obtain the warmth they need, but you can't. Sunbathing may be pleasant, but it adds nothing to your energy stores.

The continuous efficient operation of your life functions under all circumstances depends on the maintenance of your body heat at normal level.

Your body produces heat by breaking down food, and by muscular movement, and if this heat is continually given off without any regulation, chilling will occur. The greater the difference between the temperature of your body and the environment, the more rapidly this happens. (Conversely, in very hot climatic conditions, if body heat is not given off, the temperature of the body may rise to a point where collapse may occur.)

UNDERSTAND HEAT LOSS AND PREVENT EXPOSURE

The extremities of the body – your feet, hands, head, and also arms and legs to a lesser extent – are the main body heat 'radiators', and the heat they give off is conveyed to them by the circulation of the blood.

Deep within the body the blood obtains heat energy, and as it circulates it carries this heat to the extremities where it is given up to the environment **unless the extremities are insulated**. Having lost its extra heat load, the *cooled* blood returns to the deep parts of the body where more heat is absorbed, and the heat-exchange cycle is repeated. (Refrigerators and car radiators work on this principle – circulating fluid transfers heat from one area to another.)

If **body heat is given off continuously without regulation**, rapid chilling occurs because:

1. The heat loss exceeds the supply
   and
2. Chilled blood returning to the deep parts of the body cools it internally.

Under normal climatic conditions, heat gains and losses are regulated by the body, and clothes help insulate it. But, if your clothing becomes wet, or is not thick enough to provide warmth and insulation there is a continuous unbalanced heat loss – **deep chilling of the body (hypothermia) will occur** – and exposure will result.

EXPOSURE AND YOU

If you are a **solo survivor**, exposure is an **injury you can't treat yourself**, unless it is in a very mild form, because you will be too weak to help yourself – or even unconscious. So you must make every effort to avoid becoming a victim of the condition.

The symptoms of exposure are:

> **Pale, cold skin**
> **Tired and listless feeling**
> **Confusion and irrational behaviour**
> **Pulse rate slow and irregular**
> **Stumbling gait**
> **Breathing slow and laboured**
> **Swelling of hands and feet**

But it is difficult to recognize them yourself, and the best treatment is to prevent exposure occurring.

Protecting yourself against exposure is important at any time when you are in the outdoors, but in a survival situation it becomes vital – particularly if you find yourself unprepared in unexpectedly adverse climatic conditions.

CONSERVING BODY HEAT

Your first line of defence against exposure is your **clothing**, followed closely by **shelter**.

Still air is a very efficient insulator and clothing can help prevent heat loss from the body by trapping this still air close to the body, or between layers of clothing. Various factors can prevent it doing its job effectively, and these factors must be considered at all times if the maximum advantage is to be gained from clothing.

1. Bellows Action

Clothing which is not held snugly against the body and which flaps in the wind may expel warm insulating air by acting as a bellows. Try to prevent this as much as possible without making clothes so tight that they restrict movement.

2. Convection

To preserve the warmth obtained by the insulating effect of trapped air it is important that it be disturbed as little as possible. Since warm air rises, it will escape at the neck, and this warm air loss will be hastened if the air is being 'pumped' out by excessive movement of clothing in the wind.

In cold conditions you should make sure that:

Clothing is closed at the neck,
Sleeves are rolled down and fastened securely at the wrists,
Trouser legs are wrapped securely round ankles, and socks are rolled up over them to hold them in place.

WIND BLOWING THROUGH CLOTHING

Wind blowing through clothing, particularly if the clothes you are wearing do not have a close weave, disturbs the still air and destroys its insulating value. This effect is reduced if you have a wind-proof coat or jacket, but if you have no coat some plastic sheeting or paper – even newspaper – put under your shirt or jersey is almost as good, even if not as comfortable.

ALLOW SWEAT TO ESCAPE

If you are active in cold weather, and your clothes are efficient enough to retain warm air, you may start to sweat. **It is most important that you do not allow clothing to become soaked with sweat** – as to do so may increase your risk of exposure: the evaporating sweat will rob you of your body heat. Regulate the flow of warm air from your clothing at the neck and, if working very hard, allow a current of air to enter beneath a shirt or other garment by not tucking it in to your trousers top.

WET CLOTHING IS A HEAT THIEF

The insulating properties of clothing which is damp, or saturated with water, are seriously reduced. Clothing becomes wet if you sweat a lot, in rain, fog, melting snow or sleet, by immersion in water and, in every case, the result is the same: the protective value of the clothing against heat loss is very low.

Evaporation of water – the change from liquid to vapour – requires a considerable amount of heat energy, and a source of heat must be present. **If you are wearing wet clothing, you provide the source of heat energy the water needs to change to vapour, and as it changes it does a very** good job of robbing you of your body heat. (In some hot countries, practical use of this cooling effect of evaporation is used to cool water, even in the hot sun. A container of water with its surface continually wet loses heat so rapidly through evaporation of the water from the surface that the water in the container is reduced in temperature to less than the temperature of the surrounding air.)

Wind blowing through wet clothing speeds up the heat loss, and chilling can take place rapidly. (Lick the back of your hand, then blow on the wet area – the cooling effect is obvious.) The greater the wind speed, the greater the heat loss, and **exposure symptoms can be produced by the evaporation of water from clothing in a very short time.**

Any one of the three factors may not necessarily be bad by itself. Cold, particularly **dry cold,** may be uncomfortable, but is not a serious hazard. Being wet may not be too

Cold + Wet + Wind

= the formula for EXPOSURE!

Fig. 8

uncomfortable either, if the temperature is high and there is little wind. It is when cold and moisture are associated with wind that **exposure** becomes an ever-present danger.

Guard against wet clothing at all times – regardless of whether the wetting agent is climatic conditions or your own sweat. If your clothing should become saturated with water it should be removed and as much moisture as possible wrung out of it before putting it on again. This applies to wet socks, too – prolonged periods with wet, cold feet can produce a nasty condition called **trench foot,** which can cripple. If you cannot avoid wet, cold feet, use the same technique as for the prevention of frost-bite – wriggling toes and exercising the feet at regular intervals.

PROTECTION AGAINST EXPOSURE

In a survival situation where you may be completely unprepared for adverse weather conditions, it is absolutely vital that you keep the **exposure formula – (Cold + Wet + Wind = Exposure)** – firmly in your mind.

Once the factors which cause heat loss are present it becomes vitally important to seek **shelter of some kind** – no matter how primitive it may be.

Immediate shelter may not be easy to find, but even such a simple action as moving to the lee side (opposite of windward) of a mountain ridge may provide a surprising amount of protection. Rock caves, and rocky overhangs at the base of cliffs, particularly in coastal areas, and large, jumbled rocks piled up on top of each other may sometimes provide excellent shelter. (See Chapter 4, Protection.) In forested areas, shelter is not as difficult to find as it is on a bare mountainside, and even the protection given by the trunk of a fallen tree may be substantial. Immediate shelter in snow can be obtained by using the snow itself: a hole burrowed in the snow, with a wall made from the removed snow pushed up on the windward side will give a surprising amount of protection.

EXERCISE

Once shelter has been found, vigorous exercise, such as arm slapping, should be carried out to generate warmth by muscular activity. Lack of activity is a hazard which must be avoided, and when you remain in one place it is easy to succumb to the temptation to do nothing.

THE PARAMOUNT RULE

If you are caught out unprepared in bad weather conditions, there is one simple rule to remember – seek
shelter and wait. No matter how tedious it may seem.

4. Protection

In the five-point survival formula – **P–F–A–W–F** (page 12) – '**P**' is the key letter to help you remember the importance of **protection** against any adverse effects the climate or weather may have on your health and strength.

'Protection' also means defence against attack, and if you fear that wild animals may be a threat, or you need added confidence while facing the unknown, then a weapon is a great comfort – no matter how rare you may have been told animal attacks are, or how groundless are fears of the unknown.

PROTECTION BY FIRE

Apart from your clothing, which is your first line of defence against the environment (see page 37 for efficient clothing 'management'), an essential survival tool is fire.

If you can light a fire under any conditions your confidence and morale are increased enormously. The way the fire is built can vary considerably depending on the use for which the fire is intended – warmth, comfort, cooking, signalling – but it is of no use at all if you can't start it or it won't burn.

If you are in a **survival situation** while you are reading this, and you urgently need information on fire-lighting, then what follows will help you. If it is under rather more pleasant conditions, then prepare now by practising some, or all, of the techniques described – a survival situation isn't really the best time to learn fire-making techniques.

FIRE-MAKING AND FIRE-LIGHTING METHODS

Ever since man discovered fire, he has also known that it has a natural enemy – water.

To start a fire from natural materials you must have dry fuel.

Normally inflammable materials which are merely damp – and not necessarily soaking – may resist all attempts at making them burn if you try to use them for starting a fire. This doesn't say that *all* fuel for your fire must be dry, though it helps if you do have a supply of dry firewood to keep a fire going. The important thing to remember is that **dry starting material is the best guarantee of success.** No matter how impatient you may be to get a fire going, it is always worth spending time organizing your fire first. You will only waste matches, or whatever other method you are using to produce a flame (see below) if the fire is badly laid, and nothing is more frustrating and energy-consuming than spending more valuable time starting again.

Requirements for a 'Success' Fire

A suitable site where the fire is to be lit, together with materials for making a fireplace. The latter are not always easy to find, but fortunately there are a variety of methods that can be used.

    Tinder – this is the most precious part of your fire-starting materials and, although not always necessary, is essential if you are lighting a fire without matches or cigarette lighter.

    Tinder Materials include wood dust – a good source of

this finely powdered wood is the product made by wood-boring insects. It can often be found if you search round and under old dead trees; dry (very dry) powdered grass; unravelled rope or string; teased out threads from clothing

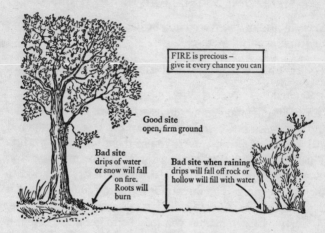

Fig. 9 *Choosing the best site for a fire*

or bandages; pocket-fluff (the bottoms of coat pockets often yield surprising amounts); bird-nest materials (particularly *old* nests) and bird feathers; and charred cotton materials. This tinder is the best for coaxing sparks into eventual flame. It is very fragile, and must be carried in a container. (See page 51.)

Kindling – You can light a fire without tinder, but you must have kindling. This should include small thin dead twigs, about the thickness of a wooden match. Whenever you get the chance you should collect such twigs. Generally driest and most inflammable if collected from dead bushes and dead branches of trees, and not from the ground. It should also include dry grass (particularly stalks) and palm and tree-fern fronds; dry bark (shredded into strips); paper money and photographs; paper – any variety – and book pages (crumpled).

Finally, there are **fire sticks**, which are 'manufactured' kindling. To make these, a knife or razor blade is essential. Particularly when starting a fire in the rain, the small amount of time required to make three or four of these sticks will repay your efforts – but they're even worth making when it's not raining.

Make them as shown, if necessary whittling away the wet outer layers of a piece of dead branch until the dry interior is reached.

If it is raining and any shelter is available, however slight, then you should try to protect your fire sticks from direct rain while you are making them. Often a dry area may be found under a fallen tree where the trunk is held up

hold this end in your hand when lighting

insert tinder under here if available

Fig. 10 Fire sticks

off the ground by the branches. Or if there is no suitable shelter, you may have to crouch over the sticks while you are making them and shield them with your own body, or a large piece of bark stripped from a tree may be used to give temporary protection from rain.

Tinder and kindling should be kept as dry as possible and really dry kindling twigs should be put under your clothing to make sure they are kept dry.

Fire-making

When you have selected the site for your fire, clear the ground of any ground litter or material which may burn for a metre or so all round the area where the fireplace is to be built.

This is particularly important in very dry conditions in forest areas when the ground litter may all be in an inflammable state.

Forest fires are frightening and very dangerous. It is hard enough being a survivor without creating extra hazards to overcome.

Make a fireplace from whatever natural materials are available and try to arrange your fireplace so that there is a base for the fire to burn on. Do not light it directly on the ground because moisture may smother the fire. A good base is particularly important if the ground is wet, and of course if you are lighting a fire on snow-covered ground then you must lay down a base first. Thick branches placed side by side will generally make a good base – even on thick snow.

Gather a *plentiful supply* of firewood *before* you light your fire. Try to have various thicknesses of fuel, ranging from sticks about finger-thickness to substantial logs. Dry sticks which are too long for placing directly on the fire, but which are light enough to handle, can often be broken into shorter lengths by grasping one end, raising in the air and then bringing down sharply on to a log, rock or the ground. If you have a knife, make two cuts in the piece of wood before you hit it against a rock. (Both methods are shown in

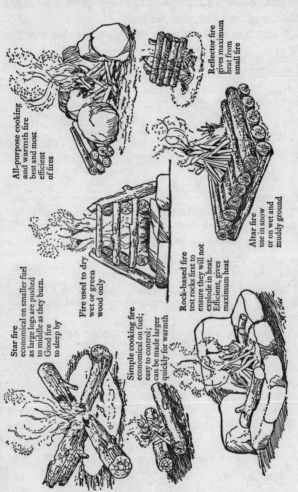

Star fire economical on smaller fuel as large logs are pushed to middle as they burn. Good fire to sleep by

All-purpose cooking and warmth fire best and most efficient of fires

Reflector fire gives maximum heat from small fire

Fire used to dry wet or green wood only

Simple cooking fire economical on fuel; easy to control; can be made larger quickly for warmth

Rock-based fire test rocks first to ensure they will not explode in heat. Efficient, gives maximum heat

Altar fire use in snow or on wet and muddy ground

Fig. 11 Fires and fireplaces

the diagram below.) Large poles can very quickly be made into short lengths using this method.

A log which is too long to handle or to cut this way can

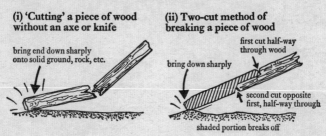

(i) 'Cutting' a piece of wood without an axe or knife

bring end down sharply onto solid ground, rock, etc.

(ii) Two-cut method of breaking a piece of wood

first cut half-way through wood

bring down sharply

second cut opposite first, half-way through

shaded portion breaks off

Fig. 12

often be reduced to a convenient manageable size by lighting a fire at its centre.

With all the necessary starting materials close by your fireplace, you are ready to light your fire.

Hold a handful of dry thin sticks in your hand as shown and, if you have some suitable tinder, push it into the end of the bundle. If you are using fire sticks, hold them by the

bundle of dry twigs

insert tinder here if available

Fig. 13

end away from the shaved 'curls' – the flame then travels up the stick, and push any small pieces of available tinder under the curled shavings.

Apply the match flame to the end of the bundle or to the sticks, then turn the whole handful until the flames have gained a good hold.

Now lay the burning twigs in your fireplace and carefully add pieces of kindling in a tepee shape. Gradually add more sticks until you are confident that the fire is well alight and has passed the nursing stage.

When your fire is underway you can build it to the size you require, and even put damp or wet fuel on it once it is well established.

Signal fires – these are a special type of fire and are described in detail in Chapter 5 (page 78).

Lighting Materials

Matches Dry matches, in a waterproof container, are without doubt one of the most useful and precious survival aids you can have. However, your supply is likely to be limited, and since you want the maximum possible there is a useful 'trick' to learn which can double your supply.

Match splitting. The ability to split matches and increase your supply is a skill worth acquiring and you can learn the technique quite easily. But it pays to practise. Also, remember that split matches, having only half a head, are very much more difficult to light successfully in a wind. (See Fig. 14 on page 50.)

Striking a split match. Once you have split a match, and thus obtained two matches, you can no longer strike them in quite the same way as a 'normal' match, since they have lost a considerable amount of their strength.

A split match must be struck by a method which stops it from breaking. It is vital that you practise this technique, too, until you can light a split match with confidence every time you try it.

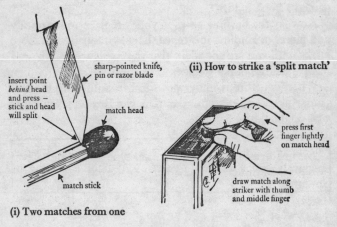

sharp-pointed knife, pin or razor blade

(ii) How to strike a 'split match'

insert point *behind* head and press — stick and head will split

match head

press first finger lightly on match head

match stick

draw match along striker with thumb and middle finger

(i) Two matches from one

Fig. 14

Method. Grasp the match about 1 cm from the head, using your thumb and middle finger, and let your first finger rest on the top of the split head.

Draw the match head along the striker, applying light pressure with your forefinger which should be *lifted as soon as the head flares.*

Flint and steel If you are in an area where *flint* is readily picked up, you have a source of fire, provided you have a steel implement with which to strike it. Flint is a dark, blue-grey stone found in chalk areas. Sparks which last long enough to be of use can be obtained by striking the piece of flint a glancing blow with the back edge of a knife (see diagram). Tinder is essential when using the flint-and-steel method, and a piece of charred cotton cloth on to which the sparks can be struck is best. Even if you have matches, and flint and steel are available, it is worth making some tinder. Char a small piece of *cotton* cloth by heating it over a fire on a piece of metal, or place it on a hot stone. Then store the charred cotton cloth carefully in a convenient container into which sparks can be struck. Suitable tinder can also be made by drying fungus sometimes found growing on trees. Dry puff balls are good tinder.

When a spark of sufficient heat strikes the tinder, it will ignite and glow over a small area. Blow on it gently and transfer it carefully to a bigger ball (about the size of your fist) of tinder material – such as wood dust, pocket fluff, dried bird nests or feathers, dry grass, bark, paper, etc. Cup the ball of tinder in your hands and blow gently into it until a flame appears. Then transfer the burning tinder to your previously prepared fire, or use it to light a bundle of kindling.

Iron pyrites and quartz Two pieces of *iron pyrites* (learn what this looks like in the mineralogy section of a museum) struck together will also produce a shower of hot sparks which will ignite prepared tinder. Pyrites will also produce sparks when struck with steel.

Quartz pebbles when struck together also produce sparks, but not as effectively as *iron pyrites*.

Condys Crystals and sugar If you have a survival kit as suggested – or a first-aid kit which contains Condys Crystals you may have enough to obtain a flame, provided you also have some sugar.

The method is simple, but to be successful all the materials and equipment must be bone dry.

Once again, *prepare your fire first*, before trying to obtain a flame.

Mix approximately half a teaspoon of Condys Crystals with one teaspoon of sugar and pour the mixture carefully into a shallow depression in a piece of wood. (Cut a hollow with a knife, or bore it out with a sharp pointed stone, if necessary.)

Using a blunt pointed stick about 1 cm thick and 25–30 cm long you now have to generate enough heat by friction to ignite the mixture. Do this by putting the blunt point of

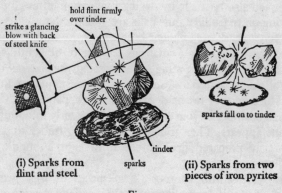

strike a glancing blow with back of steel knife

hold flint firmly over tinder

sparks fall on to tinder

tinder

sparks

(i) Sparks from flint and steel

(ii) Sparks from two pieces of iron pyrites

Fig. 15

the stick in the mixture and rotating it rapidly between the palms of your hands. The flame obtained may not last very long, but you will eventually produce a glowing coal which can be coaxed back to flame by pushing the glowing mass into a ball of tinder and blowing on it. (The drill and bow method may also be used to ignite the Condys/sugar mixture – see The Firebow – page 53.)

Magnifying glass   If the sun's rays are focused to a point with a magnifying glass the concentrated heat can light a fire. The lens or lenses removed from any of the following can be used as magnifying glasses:

Spectacles – provided the lenses are for long sight. Remove lenses and put one over the other.

Telescopes and *telescopic gun sights* – remove lenses by unscrewing lens holders from either end.

Binoculars – unscrew lenses.

Camera – if you cannot take the lens from the camera, remove or open the back; open diaphragm to its widest aperture; open shutter and keep it open by using the 'B' setting which allows the shutter to stay open as long as you push the shutter release. Then focus the sun through the lens on to prepared tinder.

Tinder is important for achieving success with a magnifying glass. The diagram shows one effective way of making a *tinder roll*. Tear a strip of cotton material from clothing, or use a bandage. Roll into a shallow cone and focus the sun into the centre of the hollow cone.

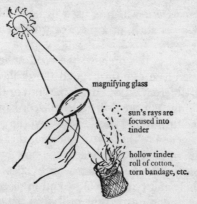

magnifying glass

sun's rays are focused into tinder

hollow tinder roll of cotton, torn bandage, etc.

Fig. 16 Producing fire with a magnifying glass

The firebow   A traditional method of producing fire is to generate heat by rubbing wood on wood. There are various ways of obtaining the necessary friction, but the easiest method, with a high chance of success, is to rotate a wooden drill in a wooden socket. The drill is rotated (while downward pressure is maintained on it) by either rolling between the palms of the hands (difficult, and needs plenty of practice), or by using a *bow*. The bow is the easiest method and provided the necessary equipment is prepared with care it is your best chance of making fire using natural materials.

Fig. 17 shows the tools and how they are assembled.

The wood from which you make the *drill-stick* should be non-resinous and as dry and hard as possible. The *base-board* should also be non-resinous and not too thick, as this would make it difficult to cut the notch in it. Pine trees are resinous – so their timber should be avoided – but any other wood may be tried, and if *willow* is available it is particularly suitable.

The *bow* can be made from any piece of dry or green branch, provided it is 'springy', i.e., when it is bent it tries to straighten out.

The *bearing-block* which is used to hold the top of the drill can be a sea shell, or a piece of wood or stone with a hollow in it.

In order to use the firebow, the cord or leather thong must first be given one turn round the drill. This can be done in two different ways. Fasten the cord or thong at both ends of the bow, put the drill under the cord and then twist it to give one turn round it. Alternatively, the cord or thong would be fastened to the bow at one end, then taken round the drill one turn, and attached to the bow by means of a loop (as shown in the diagram) or by passing the end through a hole and tying the loose end in place.

It is most important that the drill is on the *outside* of the cord or thong as shown, and that the cord or thong is upper-most on the drill on the side of the bow which will be grasped for 'sawing'. Unless you do this the drill will not operate correctly.

Make the base-board from a flat piece of wood with a shallow depression cut into it about 1 cm from one edge. On the underside of the base-board cut a Λ-shaped groove. This should extend slightly into the shallow depression.

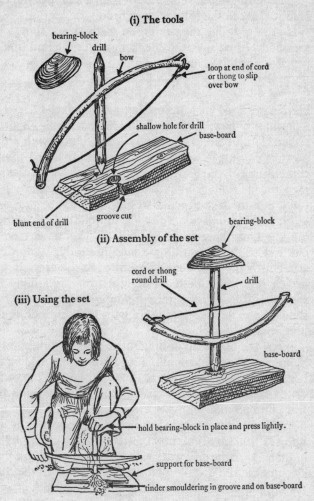

(i) The tools

bearing-block

drill

bow

loop at end of cord or thong to slip over bow

shallow hole for drill

base-board

blunt end of drill

groove cut

(ii) Assembly of the set

bearing-block

cord or thong round drill

drill

(iii) Using the set

base-board

hold bearing-block in place and press lightly.

support for base-board

tinder smouldering in groove and on base-board

Fig. 17 A fire-making set

The bearing-block should be of such a size that you can hold it easily in the palm of your hand.

If at all possible the depression in the block should be greased by using any available fat or oil, or the lead from a pencil – which is mainly graphite.

Making Fire

Having prepared your fire-making set you should have the following: a bow, complete with cord or thong; a drill, rather blunt at the bottom end; a base-board, with a depression cut just in from one edge, and a ∧-shaped groove cut underneath; a bearing-block; a supply of **tinder**; a prepared fire ready to light. With all these things assembled, you are ready to start **practising**.

There are two ways you can operate your drill: either you can kneel, one knee on the ground and your other foot on one end of the base-board to hold it steady; or you can stand with the base-board pressed against a tree. If you decide to kneel with the base-board on the ground (as shown in the diagram), then if you are right-handed you should kneel on your right knee with your left foot on the base-board.

Insert the blunt end of the drill, looped with the cord or thong, in the depression in the base-board, and holding the bearing-block in the left hand, place it over the top of the drill. Brace your left wrist against your left lower leg to give you a firm position for the bearing-block. Now, with the end of the bow held in the right hand, 'saw' it backwards and forwards. If you have the tension correctly adjusted on the cord or thong, then the drill will rotate as you move the bow from side to side. If it doesn't rotate, slacken or tighten the cord. Do not push down too hard on the bearing-block at first.

Smoke should start to come from the base-board and a fine, dark powder should start forming round the depression. This powder is what you are aiming to produce, since as the heat increases it will eventually start to smoulder, and then form a glowing coal.

If no powder appears to be forming, then a little sand or charcoal may help, if it is sprinkled around the tip of the drill. Don't overdo this. When you are able to achieve *smoke* and *wood powder* you are ready to try for fire.

Place some tinder underneath the ∧-shaped groove, and extend it out in front of the base-board a little way, as shown in the diagram.

Rotate the drill until smoke is obtained and plenty of wood powder is being formed. At this stage, increase the pressure on the bearing-block (thus increasing the pressure of the drill on the base-board) and raise the speed of the bow strokes. After about two dozen strokes, lift the drill out of the hole and quickly fold the extra tinder over the entrance to the ∧-shaped groove. Blow gently into the groove, and if smoke continues to rise, you will know that you have obtained a glowing 'fire-coal'. Wrap the tinder round the base-board so that the hole and the groove are covered, then continue to blow gently until you are rewarded with a flame.

Once you do obtain a flame, quickly transfer the tinder to a further supply, blow gently to ignite, and then apply to your prepared fire.

Don't despair if your first attempts don't produce the results you expect. You may not choose the right wood for the drill and base-board the first time you try, but keep experimenting and you will soon find that you will be rewarded with fire!

A SURVIVAL WEAPON

One of the most effective weapons you can make in a short time is a spear, and even if you don't need it to fend off wild

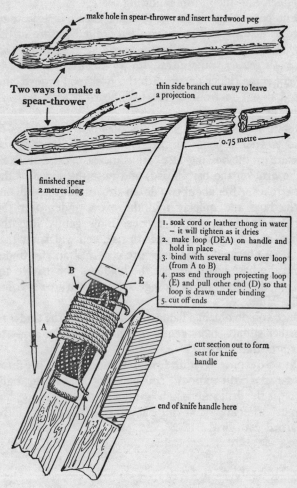

make hole in spear-thrower and insert hardwood peg

Two ways to make a spear-thrower

thin side branch cut away to leave a projection

0.75 metre

finished spear 2 metres long

1. soak cord or leather thong in water – it will tighten as it dries
2. make loop (DEA) on handle and hold in place
3. bind with several turns over loop (from A to B)
4. pass end through projecting loop (E) and pull other end (D) so that loop is drawn under binding
5. cut off ends

B

E

A

D

cut section out to form seat for knife handle

end of knife handle here

Fig. 18 Making a spear and spear-thrower

animals, it does increase your chances of killing small animals, fish and ground-birds for food.

Fig. 18 shows the method you can use to make your **spear,** and a **spear-thrower** also, if you want to hunt in true native style. To ensure that your spear 'flies true' it is important that the knife, or whatever you use for a point, is fastened at the *heavy butt end* of the spear shaft. Unless you do this your spear will turn end over end when you throw it and is unlikely to penetrate your target.

THROWING YOUR SPEAR

Before throwing your spear at anything, remember that the knife fastened to it is a very important piece of equipment, and to lose it could be a minor disaster.

To throw accurately, rest the spear on your shoulder and hurl it forward using your forearm as a lever. Accuracy can be increased if you use a spear-thrower, and you will find

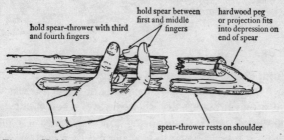

hold spear-thrower with third and fourth fingers

hold spear between first and middle fingers

hardwood peg or projection fits into depression on end of spear

spear-thrower rests on shoulder

Fig. 19 Holding a spear and spear-thrower before throwing

that you can also throw farther and with greater force if you make and use this simple device which has been used by hunters for hundreds of years.

It is placed on your shoulder and held together with the spear as shown in the diagram. Note the position of the fingers and how they hold the spear and the thrower.

Even if your spear is never used for your own protection it does give you one further advantage – it increases your reach, and if it is 2 metres in length it means you can easily reach up with it at arm's length to as much as 4 metres or more. This is quite an advantage for dislodging fruit or berries otherwise difficult to obtain.

SHELTER

Shelter in survival conditions is anything other than clothing which provides a barrier between yourself and the elements.

It can be extremely simple – getting on to the lee side of a mountain ridge away from the wind, is an example – or it can be a relatively complex, weatherproof structure, built entirely from natural materials.

As a survivor, you should always be on the lookout for possible natural shelter, or materials from which a shelter can be constructed.

NATURAL SHELTERS

Natural shelter is sometimes provided by

1. *Large, fallen trees* If the trunk of a fallen tree is very large, it may provide a dry, sheltered area where it curves up from the ground. It is surprising how little space is required for a person lying down to be sheltered by a horizontal log, and this form of protection should not be neglected. If there are hollows in the ground under a large, fallen tree trunk, or the trunk is not right down on the ground, then the chances of finding dry shelter are even better.

2. *Caves* These may sometimes be found in mountainous country and are very common in limestone areas. Without proper equipment, it is unwise to venture far into obviously

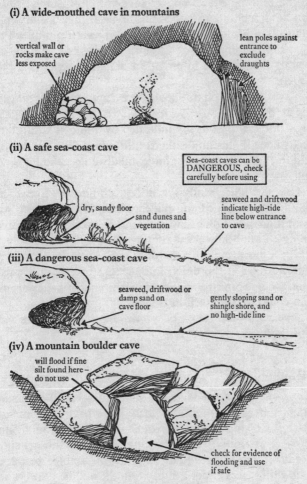

(i) A wide-mouthed cave in mountains

vertical wall or
rocks make cave
less exposed

lean poles against
entrance to
exclude
draughts

(ii) A safe sea-coast cave

Sea-coast caves can be
DANGEROUS, check
carefully before using

dry, sandy floor

sand dunes and
vegetation

seaweed and driftwood
indicate high-tide
line below entrance
to cave

(iii) A dangerous sea-coast cave

seaweed, driftwood or
damp sand on
cave floor

gently sloping sand or
shingle shore, and
no high-tide line

(iv) A mountain boulder cave

will flood if fine
silt found here –
do not use

check for evidence of
flooding and use
if safe

Fig. 20 Natural shelters

large caves, and it is better to look for a dry floor area as near to the cave mouth as possible. Very wide-mouthed caves can be draughty and rather cold, even if they are dry, but quite often boulders can be piled up as a vertical wall which meets the sloping wall of the cave, or poles can be stood up against the entrance to provide a draught barrier (see Fig. 20 (i)).

Caves on **sea coasts** should be examined with *great* care before deciding to use them as shelter. Always look for the high-tide mark, generally indicated by a line of seaweed or driftwood. If this line extends into a cave (see Fig. 20 (ii) and (iii)), then the sea will undoubtedly enter it and it is not suitable as shelter.

Caves with flat, sandy beaches extending away from them should be examined for evidence of invasion by the sea, even if no high-tide line is apparent. Seaweed inside a cave, or damp sand only a few centimetres below the surface of the cave floor, indicates that it is unlikely to be a safe, dry shelter. Also, if the beach leading to a cave is rather flat, then the tide can advance very quickly, and without warning you could find yourself in trouble.

Avoid sea-coast caves, unless you are absolutely sure they are not entered by the sea.

BOULDER CAVES

Large masses of boulders are sometimes found in mountainous areas, or in valleys where there have been ancient glaciers which have since retreated. Landslides from mountains down into river valleys (which have subsequently become forested) are often composed of jumbled blocks of rock with spaces under and between them. These spaces are sometimes big enough to provide dry shelter (see Fig. 20 (iv)), but before you enthusiastically adopt such a space as 'home', always ensure that it is not in an area which will

flood following the rise of a stream or river, or the floor consists of a hollow which will fill with water after heavy rain.

Check for flooding by looking for water lines on the
boulders – a straight, muddy line is very suspicious – or the
presence of fine silt on the ground or in the moss growing
under or on the rock. Avoid these areas.

If you can be sure of your safety in such a shelter they can
often give very comfortable, secure weatherproof protection, especially if a fire is lit at the entrance to the
opening.

BIVOUACS

A 'bivouac' is a temporary shelter and is built entirely from
natural materials. It can provide very satisfactory protection against even the harshest weather conditions.

It can be simple or elaborate, depending on how long you
intend to use it but, regardless of the length of time it is to
be in use, there are certain features you should consider
before starting work.

Building Time

Unless the preparation of a bivouac is suddenly forced on
you (see Emergency Bivouac, page 66), it is important that
you allow yourself adequate time, with plenty of daylight,
since it often takes much longer than you would think to
gather the materials and to build a shelter.

Choosing a Site

Ideally, the site for a bivouac should satisfy several requirements. The first two of the following list are *absolutely*
essential.

1. Solid, preferably high ground, free from mud and out of
   what are possibly dry watercourses or flood levels of
   streams or rivers.

2. Ample materials for building the bivouac.
3. Ample dry firewood.
4. Proximity to water.

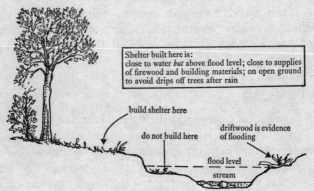

Shelter built here is:
close to water *but* above flood level; close to supplies
of firewood and building materials; on open ground
to avoid drips off trees after rain

build shelter here

do not build here

driftwood is evidence
of flooding

flood level

stream

*Fig. 21 Choosing a site for a shelter above river or stream flood
level*

Always place the greatest emphasis on condition number 1,
even if it is necessary to carry or drag your building
materials to the site. The diagram overleaf shows a
simple but effective bivouac requiring the minimum of
materials to achieve adequate shelter. Although it is open on
one side, this type of frame-and-thatch bivouac is much
more efficient than the type covered in on all sides.

It is easier to make, requires only half the amount of
thatching material (invariably you will gather far less than
you need) and, with a fire built on the open side, provides a
warm, dry shelter.

You will often need vines or long, fibrous roots or leaves
to bind the framework of a bivouac together and it is important that the right kind of knots are used to tie or join

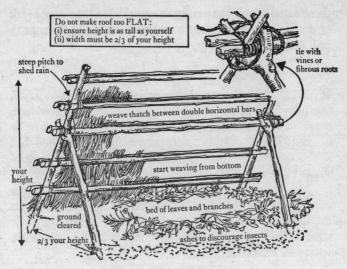

Do not make roof too FLAT:
(i) ensure height is as tall as yourself
(ii) width must be 2/3 of your height

tie with vines or fibrous **roots**

steep pitch to shed rain

weave thatch between double horizontal bars

start weaving from bottom

your height

bed of leaves and branches

ground cleared

2/3 your height

ashes to discourage insects

Fig. 22 Lean-to bivouac shelter

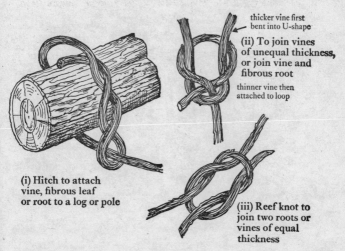

thicker vine first bent into U-shape

(ii) To join vines of unequal thickness, or join vine and fibrous root

thinner vine then attached to loop

(i) Hitch to attach vine, fibrous leaf or root to a log or pole

(iii) Reef knot to join two roots or vines of equal thickness

Fig. 23 Simple knots to tie or join vines, fibrous leaves and roots

these materials. If the wrong knots are used they may break or cut themselves on their own knots when you attempt to pull them tight. See Fig. 23.

Emergency Bivouac

If you have to prepare a shelter *without any equipment at all*, the following procedure should be followed. If you have some means of lighting a fire quickly with matches or cigarette lighter, your problem is considerably lessened, but if you don't have these (you would, if you carried a survival kit), then your preparations would *start at point 4*.

This is the type of shelter to make if time is short, the weather is turning bad, or you are caught out in the bush in the dark (in these circumstances and if you lack any other kind of illumination, a fire will be necessary for you to see what you are doing).

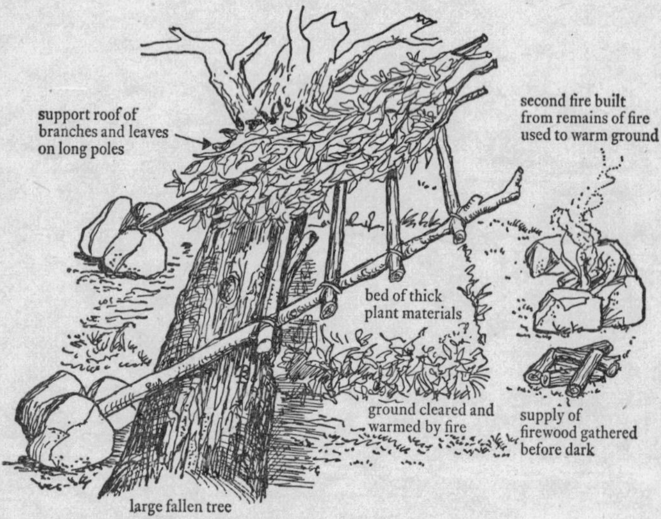

support roof of branches and leaves on long poles

second fire built from remains of fire used to warm ground

bed of thick plant materials

ground cleared and warmed by fire

supply of firewood gathered before dark

large fallen tree

Fig. 24 An emergency bivouac

1. Find a sound, fallen tree, on level ground, if possible, or a large rock. (If neither of these can be found, you may have to use a Lopped-Tree Bivouac – see page 68.)

   Select the side of the log or rock where you intend to make your bed, clear away any ground litter, and light a good, roaring fire *on this spot* to dry it out and heat the ground. (If you light the fire near a log and the bark catches fire it can be extinguished with a handful of dirt. But beware of lighting your fire near a hollow or decayed log, because once alight it will be much harder to extinguish.)

2. While the fire is burning, collect as much firewood as possible and pile it up near your shelter site. (Always gather much more than you think you need – it's better to have too much than not enough.)

3. When the fire has been burning for about half an hour or more, push all the embers out with a couple of sticks to about $1\frac{1}{2}$ metres from the log. Make sure no burning embers are left where your bed is to be.

   With the burning embers from the first fire, build your main fire for the night, using any rocks or short logs available behind it to act as heat reflectors.

   (If you haven't been able to start a fire, proceed from here.)

4. Cover the ground where you have had the fire with a deep layer of leafy branches stripped from trees or bushes; fern leaves; moss or grass. *This layer of plant material is your bed*, and the deeper it is the warmer you will be, since it will keep you well clear of the ground.

5. If you lie on the bed of plant material as close to the log as possible, it will shelter you extremely effectively, and with a well-built fire the warmth generated against the log will keep you comfortable, even on a cold night.

   For extra protection, you can heap extra plant material on top of yourself since the greater the amount of still

air that is trapped around you, the lower the heat loss.
6. *Protection against rain*   If there is a possibility of rain, then some kind of a roof should be erected to protect you directly above without interfering with the heat from your fire. The diagram shows one way of doing this by laying poles over the log from the side opposite from where you intend to sleep so that they form a sloping framework. Cover them as thickly as possible with plant materials or leafy branches, butt ends upwards, and you will make an effective lean-to roof.

Lopped-Tree Bivouac

An axe or machete will be necessary if you are to make this type of shelter, but it is a quick method to make a shelter from a small, leafy tree. Choose a tree approximately 3 metres high and partially cut through its trunk at about half

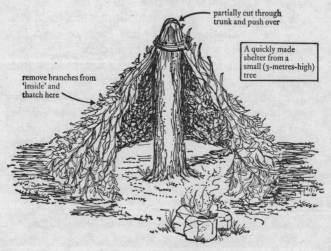

partially cut through trunk and push over

A quickly made shelter from a small (3-metres-high) tree

remove branches from 'inside' and thatch here

Fig. 25 A lopped-tree bivouac

its height. Push the top of the tree over so that the top is on the ground while the stem is still attached to the butt. Cut or tear away the branches on the 'inside' to use as thatching on the outside. Break any upstanding branches on the outside so that they hang down. Thatch the shelter with the boughs removed from the inside, together with material gathered from other trees and bushes.

Light a fire in front of this den-like shelter – and don't forget a bed on the ground.

SHELTER IN THE SNOW

When faced with survival in snow country there is no need to despair, even if the situation does seem to require desperate measures.

Travelling in snow, particularly if you are ill-equipped for such conditions, can rapidly lead to exhaustion, and in soft snow the amount of energy expended is considerable (see A Sapling Snow Shoe, page 131).

It is even more important in snow conditions that you allow yourself plenty of time to prepare a shelter, and particularly that you do not allow yourself to become so cold and exhausted that you are incapable of making a suitable shelter.

This is a vital consideration. If you are a survivor in snow conditions you must prepare shelter before exhaustion robs you of the necessary energy.

Snow itself is a source of shelter, and the most primitive snow shelter – a hole burrowed into a drift and then blocked up so that it is *almost sealed off* from the outside world – can be almost comfortable, particularly if something is available as insulation for you to sit or lie on, such as a rucksack, parka or anorak, piece of plastic or tree branches, even a piece of cardboard or paper. Note that any snow burrow should be *almost* sealed off – **not** completely sealed off from the outside world. This is because the air in a small shelter will soon become stale and unfit to breathe.

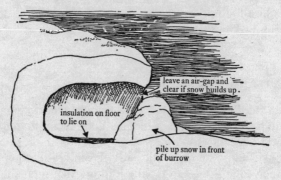

leave an air-gap and clear if snow builds up.

insulation on floor to lie on

pile up snow in front of burrow

Fig. 26 A burrow in a snow drift

Because air is trapped in snow it makes a surprisingly efficient insulator and *heat-trap*, but this ability to trap heat can cause trouble. If you are in a snow burrow or snow cave for any length of time your body heat will cause the snow of the walls and floor to thaw and become slushy. This is another reason for making sure you use anything you have to sit or lie on. If you have a rucksack, it should be used as a sort of half sleeping bag into which you put your feet. Remember also that spare socks make good gloves.

SHELTER IN A SNOW HOLE

In forest areas under snow, even deep snow, you will find some trees where the wind swirling round the trunk has left a depression in the snow. This depression can be enlarged

into a **snow hole** (see Fig. 28) and by breaking branches
from the tree, or other trees, it can be made into an efficient
and comfortable shelter.

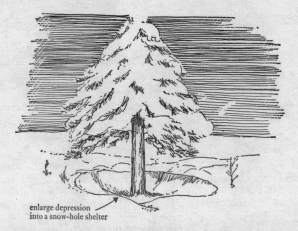

enlarge depression
into a snow-hole shelter

Fig. 27 A depression in snow around a tree trunk

In deep packed snow in forest country, a trench can be
dug and the snow from it heaped up on one side, as
shown in Fig. 29. It can also offer very good protection if
branches are used to form a roof over the trench, and a
coating of snow is thrown on top. *Note* – the branches
placed inside so that you are not lying directly on the snow,
and also the vertical pole, to allow an air-hole to be kept
open.

The type of shelter shown in Fig. 30 really requires
some kind of digging implement, and if you are lucky
enough to have something to dig with, this 'improved'
shelter can be constructed. Note once again the bedding,
and the pole to keep the air-hole open.

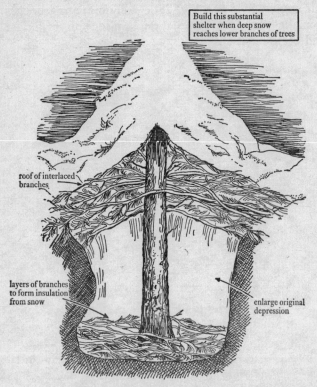

Build this substantial
shelter when deep snow
reaches lower branches of trees

roof of interlaced
branches

layers of branches
to form insulation
from snow

enlarge original
depression

Fig. 28 An enlarged snow-hole shelter in deep snow

(*Reminder*: Working hard to build a snow shelter can cause you to *sweat*. Read Chapter 3 – Exposure – again. It will help to fix in your mind that sweating in very cold conditions must be controlled.)

Shelter is a barrier between you and the elements, and protection is what you achieve when you build a shelter.

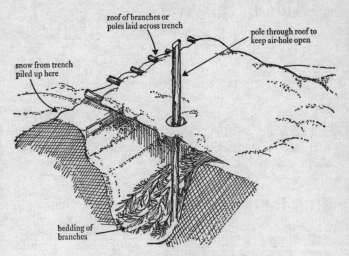

roof of branches or
poles laid across trench

pole through roof to
keep air-hole open

snow from trench
piled up here

bedding of
branches

Fig. 29 A simple snow-trench shelter

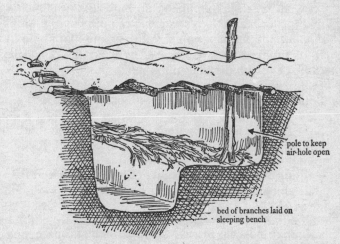

pole to keep
air-hole open

bed of branches laid on
sleeping bench

Fig. 30 Improved snow shelter made with a digging implement

5. Aids in Survival

'A' is the initial letter for *Aids* in the survival formula, and *A*ids are *A*nything that you can use to ensure your survival, maintain your health and strength, and bring about your return to civilization.

SIGNALLING FOR HELP

Attracting attention to yourself and your situation is an important aid in your survival repertoire.

If you – are a survivor from any kind of disaster such as an aircraft crash or shipwreck/become lost through separation from an organized group on an outdoor expedition/are overdue for return to civilization after a definite date which is known to someone – **you should assume that a search is in progress for you** and all your actions should be carried out with that thought in mind.

Someone cares and someone is looking for you.

So – if you are a survivor from any disaster and you are cut off from civilization, remember

– **all aircraft should be regarded as search aircraft**
– **all ships and boats should be regarded as rescue vessels**

and every possible means should be used to make your presence known to any possible human contact.

Always keep this thought in your mind – the human race has a built-in urge to respond to people in distress, but you must inform searchers, or people who don't even know you are in trouble, that **you are in distress** and unless you come face-to-face with possible rescuers then there is only one way you can do so – you must use **distress signals.**

CALLING FOR HELP

The most obvious method of attracting attention is to use your voice. As a distress signal, your voice has a very serious drawback, however. If you use it too much or put too much effort into trying for maximum sound, you not only get a sore throat but your method of signalling becomes worn out! Obviously, you can't shout to aeroplanes, or call across large distances of water and calling in isolated places is un-likely to be of use unless 'listening ears' are not too far away. In thickly-forested areas the vegetation absorbs sound very effectively; and if you are going to use your voice to attract attention you must use a better method than shouting. It is possible to use your voice as a method of signalling which also leaves your voice intact. The method involves using the two words '**far**' and '**call**'.

'FAR-CALLING'

The problem with shouting is that the duration of the sound is short and anyone listening for, or hearing, a shout often finds it difficult to locate the direction from which the sound is coming.

Producing a continuous sound by using the technique of far-calling largely overcomes these difficulties.

How to Attract Attention Using Your Voice
1. Take a deep breath.
   Then

2. Produce the drawn-out sound **fah-ah-ah-ah** with a steady exhalation of your breath.
3. This drawn-out 'far' sound is now linked to the second part of the signal which is the word 'call'. So
4. When you have used nearly all your breath on **fah-ah-ah-ah** – take another deep breath and change the sound to a drawn-out **cor-orl**. Thus the total sound signal in two breaths is:

(Breath) – Fah-ah-ah-ah- (Breath) – Cor-or-orl

The long continuous sound obtained from a 'far-call' will travel a considerable distance, and if you cup your hands round your mouth to form a 'trumpet' the distance it will be heard will be increased even more. Remember to repeat the call every so often.

Coo-ee

Coo-ee is a famous Australian voice signal and it is given in the same way as a far-call, except that one breath is sufficient. About half your breath should be used on the drawn-out 'coo' sound, and the other half on a drawn-out 'ee' sound.

A 'coo-ee' sound travels a surprisingly long way.

Whistle

A whistle is excellent for attracting attention and has the added advantage that it saves your voice. If you have a survival kit complete with whistle (see page 14) which can be attached to your clothing, then you should tie it to a convenient buttonhole or pin it where it can be reached easily. Not only does this save a valuable aid from being lost, but it can be held in your mouth, leaving both hands free for making your way through thick vegetation or feeling your way in the dark.

FLASHING SIGNALS

Many survivors have been located and rescued because they attracted attention simply by reflecting the sun off a shiny object – such as a mirror, can lid, knife blade or any piece of polished metal. Without some method of aiming such a signal at your target, it is difficult to be sure that it is in fact arriving where you want it to arrive. The answer to this problem is solved if you use a heliograph with a sighting device, as described on pages 18–20.

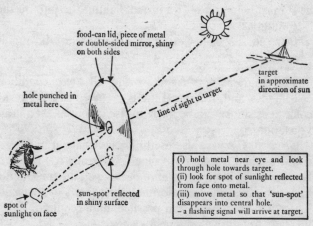

Fig. 31 To send a flashing signal

There is another answer to the sighting problem, and if you have a piece of metal such as a can lid, which is shiny on both sides, then a different technique can be used. The diagram shows how this is done.

Remember, though – before any flashing signal can be made – the sun must be shining.

SIGNAL FIRE

Using a **signal fire** to attract attention is extremely
effective, and whenever a camp is established a signal fire
should always be prepared ready for lighting at a moment's
notice. This is particularly important if a searching aircraft
should appear.

Several points must be kept in mind when building a
signal fire:

1. It must produce a column of smoke visible for a considerable distance.
2. It must remain ready for instant lighting, despite weather
conditions.
3. Once lit, its effectiveness as a signal must be rapidly
achieved.

The diagrams opposite show how all these conditions
can be met, and, if a signal fire is prepared as described, a
column of smoke can be made to rise up out of even heavy
vegetation.
Multiple Bonfires are also useful for signalling at night, and
if this method is used *three* should be lit in a triangle. The
best plan is to have one bonfire burning all the time, and to
have two other unlit fires forming the corners of a triangle.
These two fires, covered, if possible, until required, should
be ready to light at a moment's notice.

INTERNATIONAL DISTRESS SIGNALS

Various simple distress signals are recognized and used
throughout the world. They have been specially devised for
use in emergencies, and whenever assistance is required by
a survivor of a disaster, or it is obvious that a disaster is
imminent (such as a ship sinking) then one or more of these
signals should be used.

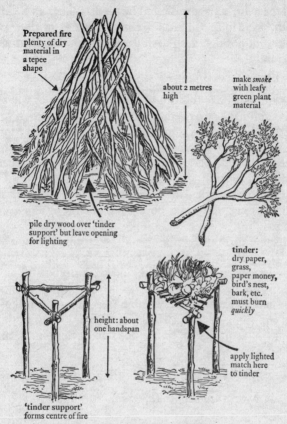

Prepared fire plenty of dry material in a tepee shape

about 2 metres high

make *smoke* with leafy green plant material

pile dry wood over 'tinder support' but leave opening for lighting

tinder: dry paper, grass, paper money, bird's nest, bark, etc. must burn *quickly*

height: about one handspan

apply lighted match here to tinder

'tinder support' forms centre of fire

Fig. 32 A signal fire

IMPORTANT: whatever kind of signal is used to supply information to searchers – particularly from the air – every possible means should also be employed to attract searchers to the area where the signals are laid out. For example, if S.O.S. is laid out on a beach with stones, then a signal fire should be built in the vicinity.

S.O.S. – this signal, which is understood everywhere to be a call for help, may be indicated by the actual letters S.O.S., or sent by Morse Code as a repeated series of dots and dashes (dot dot dot, dash dash dash, dot dot dot) in groups as follows:

··· −−− ···/··· −−− ···/··· −−− ···/etc.

A Morse signal like this can be sent with a torch or whistle, even if you have never sent a Morse message before in your life. Whether you use a torch or whistle, send your Morse S.O.S. in the groups shown, making the dots (···) *short* flashes or whistle blasts, and the dashes (−−−) *long* flashes or whistle blasts.

S.O.S. is a particularly good signal to make in snow, although it can, of course, be laid out in large letters in any situation.

In snow or sand S.O.S. should be stamped or shuffled into letters about 7–10 metres long. After the initial shapes of the letters are made, they should be enlarged and made as deep as possible so that shadows help to make them stand out. Condys Crystals, if available (see page 15), make an excellent signal when sprinkled on snow. Only a small amount is required to give a deep red colour to a large amount of snow.

Morse Code

The full Morse Code is as follows:

A	·−	J	·−−−	S	···
B	−···	K	−·−	T	−
C	−·−·	L	·−··	U	··−
D	−··	M	−−	V	···−
E	·	N	−·	W	·−−
F	··−·	O	−−−	X	−··−
G	−−·	P	·−−·	Y	−·−−
H	····	Q	−−·−	Z	−−··
I	··	R	·−·		

Numbers may be sent in Morse also:

1	·————	6	—····
2	··———	7	——···
3	···——	8	———··
4	····—	9	————·
5	·····	0	—————

Flag Distress Signal

The signal which is shown in the diagram below may be used on land, or at sea, although it is normally used on a boat.

A square 'flag' made from any material with a ball *above* or *below* it

Fig. 33 Flag distress signal

It consists of a square flag made from any material with a ball, or anything resembling a ball, above or below it.

GROUND-TO-AIR EMERGENCY SIGNALS

The signals which follow are used to convey information to aircraft and they should be laid out using any materials which

1	I	Require doctor, serious injuries	
2	II	Require medical supplies	
3	X	Unable to proceed	
4	F	Require food and water	
5	⋁	Require firearms and ammunition	
6	◇	Require map and compass	
7	I	Require signal lamp with battery, and radio	
8	K	Indicate direction to proceed	
9	↑	Am proceeding in this direction	
10	▷	Will attempt take-off	
11	⌐⌐	Aircraft seriously damaged	
12	△	Probably safe to land here	
13	L	Require fuel and oil	
14	LL	All well	
15	N	No	
16	Y	Yes	
17	⌐⌐	Not understood	
18	W	Require engineer	

Fig. 34 Ground-to-air emergency signals

will give as great a contrast as possible to the background.

Pieces of wreckage from a ship or aircraft, clothing, pieces of sails or other fabric, branches, whole shrubs or large leaves, stones – all these things may be used – or anything else that happens to be available.

Each signal should be at least $2\frac{1}{2}$ metres in length, and when a signal consists of two parts, there should be not less than 3 metres between each part.

ACKNOWLEDGEMENT FROM AIRCRAFT TO THE SURVIVOR ON THE GROUND

Message Understood

When ground signals have been seen and understood by the pilot of an aircraft he will acknowledge the message by either:

1. Rocking from side to side
   or
2. Sending a succession of green flashes from a lamp.

Message NOT Understood

Either

1. The aircraft will make a complete right-hand circuit
   or
2. A succession of red flashes from a lamp will be sent.

REPETITIVE SIGNALS

You can tell ground searchers that you are in trouble by making repetitive signals – whistle blasts, flashes with a torch, banging on an empty oil drum – all these methods are effective if searchers are in hearing range or line of sight, but the sounds must be regularly spaced with definite intervals between each. If they are not they could be confused with the sound of hunting or other noises.

The International Mountain Rescue Code signal consists of
  6 evenly spaced whistle blasts (or torch flashes) over 1
    minute – i.e., 1 blast every 10 seconds until 6 have
    been blown
followed by
  1 minute's silence
then
  6 more blasts at 10-second intervals.

The reply to this signal consists of
  3 blasts in 1 minute – i.e., 1 blast every 20 seconds for
    1 minute
followed by
  1 minute's silence
then
  3 more blasts at 20-second intervals.

INTERNATIONAL PHONETIC ALPHABET

When giving a message or position by radio or telephone, it
is important that whoever is receiving the information is not
left in any doubt as to the actual content of the message. It
is easy to confuse a letter or figure that may sound like
another (S and F, B and V, M and N, are examples), and so
an International Phonetic Alphabet and number system has
been very carefully devised. It is possible to give a whole
message using this alphabet, but since this would be tedious
and time-consuming, it is generally used only when a
doubtful spelling is involved, when it is important that the
initial letter of a word is transmitted correctly, or that a
series of numbers is correctly received. Here is 'Survivor'
given in the International Phonetic Alphabet: **Sierra
Uniform Romeo Victor India Victor Oscar Romeo.**
To ensure that there will be no confusion, each word should
be pronounced exactly as shown in the list. Figures (0–9)

have their own unusual pronunciation, and since they are so different from those you are used to it is worth practising saying them aloud.

The International Phonetic Alphabet

	Word	Pronounced as		Word	Pronounced as
A	Alfa	AL fah	N	November	No VEM ber
B	Bravo	BRAH voh	O	Oscar	OSS cah
C	Charlie	CHAR lee *or*	P	Papa	Pah PAH
		SHAR lee	Q	Quebec	Keh BECK
D	Delta	DELL tah	R	Romeo	ROW me oh
E	Echo	ECK oh	S	Sierra	See AIR rah
F	Foxtrot	FOKS trot	T	Tango	TANG go
G	Golf	Golf	U	Uniform	YOU nee form *or*
H	Hotel	Hoh TELL			OO nee form
I	India	IN dee ah	V	Victor	VIK tah
J	Juliet	JEW lee ETT	W	Whiskey	WISS key
K	Kilo	KEY loh	X	X-Ray	ECKS ray
L	Lima	LEE mah	Y	Yankee	YANG key
M	Mike	Mike	Z	Zulu	ZOO loo

Figures

	Word	Pronounced as		Word	Pronounced as
0	NadaZero	Nah-dah-zay-roh	5	Pantafive	Pan-tah-five
1	Unaone	Oo-nah-wun	6	Soxisix	Sok-see-six
2	Bissotwo	Bees-soh-too	7	Setteseven	Say-tay-seven
3	Terrathree	Tay-rah-three	8	Oktoeight	Ok-toh-ait
4	Kartefour	Kar-tay-fower	9	Novenine	No-vay-niner

Decimal point		Decimal	Day-see-mal
Full stop		Stop	Stop

MAYDAY

'Mayday' is a word known throughout the world as a distress signal indicating **grave** and **imminent danger**. It is a *spoken signal* and is used when it is possible to transmit on a radio-telephone. The information which follows gives the full procedures which are accepted everywhere whenever a ship or aircraft is in distress and human life is in danger.

Lack of knowledge of the procedures which follow need not prevent you from using Mayday as a distress call.

So – if you should ever be in a 'Mayday situation' and the necessary equipment (radio-telephone) is available, do not hesitate to use the distress call Mayday, Mayday, Mayday followed by any information (keep it simple) that you can give.

If you are able to follow the standard procedures, they are as follows:

Distress Transmitting Procedure

The 'International Code of Signals 1969' sets out the procedure to be used when **immediate assistance** is required. These are as follows:

To indicate distress

1. Send the following Distress Call: Mayday Mayday Mayday. This is . . .
   (name or call sign of ship or aircraft spoken three times).
2. Then send the Distress Message composed of:
   Mayday followed by the name or call sign of ship
   Position of ship
   Nature of distress
   And, if necessary, transmit the nature of the aid required and any other information which will help the rescue.

In case of language difficulties:

1. First send the word **Interco** to indicate that the message will be in the International Code of Signals.
2. Send the *Distress Call*:

   Mayday Mayday Mayday. This is . . . (give name or call sign of ship or aircraft, spoken three times letter by letter, and use the International Phonetic Alphabet. If any figures are involved these should be pronounced as shown.)
3. Then send the *Distress Message* composed of:

   (i) **Position** – indicate (if known) *by bearing and distance from a landmark* or *by latitude and longitude*. The following code systems for indicating position by either of these two methods are from the International Code of Signals:

   (a) *by bearing and distance from a landmark:*
   Give code letter **A (Alfa)** followed by the ship or aircraft's **true bearing** (this will be a three-figure group – see Bearings, page 102) from the landmark and **name the landmark**. Follow this by giving code letter **R (Romeo)** followed by the **distance in nautical miles** (one or more figures) from the landmark.

   (b) *by latitude and longitude:*
   Give code letter **L (Lima)** followed by **latitude** (a four-figure group – two figures for degrees, two figures for minutes) and either **N (November)** for latitude north or **S (Sierra)** for latitude south.

   Then give code letter **G (Golf)** followed by the **longitude** (a five-figure group – three figures for degrees, two figures for minutes) and either **E (Echo)** for longitude east or **W (Whiskey)** for longitude west.

(ii) **Nature of distress** – indicate this by transmitting the following code letters or words.

Code letters	Words to be transmitted	Meaning
AE	Alfa Echo	I must abandon my vessel
BF	Bravo Foxtrot	Aircraft is ditched in position indicated and requires immediate assistance
CB	Charlie Bravo	I require immediate assistance
CB6	Charlie Bravo Soxisix	I require immediate assistance, I am on fire
DX	Delta X-Ray	I am sinking
HW	Hotel Whiskey	I have collided with surface craft

Two examples of distress messages using procedures above

1. *By Bearing and Distance from a Landmark*

   (a) **Mayday Mayday Mayday** (name of ship spoken three times or call sign of ship spelt three times in phonetic alphabet)

   (b) **Mayday** . . . (name or call sign of ship) **Interco Alfa Nadazero Bissotwo Pantafive** (name of landmark) **Romeo Soxisix Nadazero Delta X-Ray**

   Meaning: (ship) in distress, message is in International Code of Signals, position 025 degrees true bearing from (landmark) 60 nautical miles from (landmark) I am sinking.

2. *By Latitude and Longitude*

   (a) **Mayday Mayday Mayday** (name of ship spoken three times or call sign of ship spelt three times in phonetic alphabet)

(b) **Mayday ... (name or call sign of ship) Interco Lima Kartefour Terrathree Nadazero Pantafive Sierra Golf Nadazero Bissotwo Pantafive Soxisix Oktoeight Echo Charlie Bravo Soxisix**
Meaning: (ship) in distress, message is in International Code of Signals, position latitude 43 05 south longitude 025 68 east I require immediate assistance, I am on fire.

FOREST LORE

Forest lore is the art of living successfully in the outdoors by turning everything in it to your own advantage.

LEARNING FOREST LORE

No one ever inherited instinctive knowledge of forest lore – it is an ability which must be learnt. Knowledge is required, but it has to combine with your powers of *observation* before it is effective.

Observation is really the foundation of forest lore and the development of this faculty pays handsome dividends. Try to cultivate the habit of observation and awareness of your surroundings at every available opportunity. If you are travelling in the countryside, or flying in an aeroplane, study the land formation and take mental note of the patterns of rivers and streams. Notice how ridges with their side spurs are all part of the drainage pattern; how main ridges often form the best routes on to mountains; how rivers and streams may sometimes lead into gorges and ravines.

Study the countryside and mentally file your observations. They can be of great assistance to you should you ever find yourself in a survival situation in mountainous or hilly country where choosing the right route may be extremely important.

ROUTE FINDING

One of the attributes of a good 'woodsman' is his ability to find and travel by the best and safest route through rough country. When you are in a heavily forested area it is even more important that the right decisions are made calmly and without panic, and it is in such circumstances that knowledge of the 'lie of the land' is even more important.

The diagram which follows illustrates an important principle of route finding. As a general rule, unless the nature of the terrain obviously prevents you from doing so – **you should travel UP spurs and mountain ridges, and DOWN streams and rivers.**

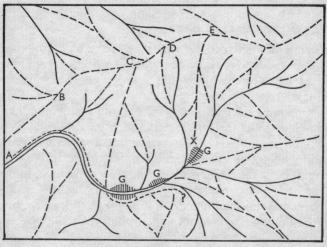

Fig. 35 Ridge travel and river following

In the diagram, a main ridge of land dividing one valley from another is shown by A–B–C–D–E. If you wish to travel from A to E there are two main alternatives. You could follow the river, but this would mean passing three gorges (G) and fording several tributaries as well as the river itself. The greatest danger, however, is the possibility of following the wrong branch of the river, and in heavily forested country this is very easy to do.

If the alternative decision is made, to follow the ridge, then not only is the distance from A to E less, but you will avoid any trouble with tributaries, crossing the river itself, or difficulty with gorges. Your vantage point will also be increased, since, as you climb upwards, you will have a clearer idea of the land pattern you are traversing.

Travelling from E to A by way of the ridge E–D–C–B–A is a much more difficult proposition, and in this case it may prove more advantageous to follow the river. If you are in a forested area, the possibility that you may stray on to side spurs (such as E–X) is very high. Unless you are extremely cautious, it could lead you into difficulties or time-consuming retracing of your route. To avoid this you can sometimes find a climbable tree which will give you a view. If this is not possible, then mark your route with care so that if necessary you can find your way back to the place where you took the wrong direction.

It is not always easy to tell which is a main ridge and which is a side spur, and when there are obviously two possibilities you should mark the spot so that it will be recognizable should you have to return to it. Various methods of route marking are set out below.

Marking Your Route

When you are travelling through a forest, particularly when it is not possible to obtain a view of the whole area, you must be able to mark your direction of travel since there is always a possibility that you may have to retrace your steps.

BLAZING A TRAIL

Blazing is a method of marking trees so that a distinctive, easily recognized mark is made. With a knife, machete or small hatchet remove a slice of bark about half a metre in length from part of the trunk which is easily visible from a distance.

Blazes should always be made on both sides of a tree, and to prevent confusion regarding your direction of travel, the **a-way/to-wards** system should be used.

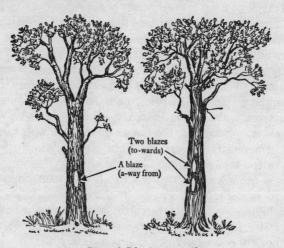

Two blazes
(to-wards)

A blaze
(a-way from)

Fig. 36 Blazing a trail

On the side of a tree which is along the general direction-line of your travel make **one blaze**, and on the side of the tree towards the direction from which you are coming make **two blazes**. If you use this system you cannot confuse your direction, since **one blaze means a-way** from your last position and **two blazes means to-wards** your last position. After making a blaze always look back to make sure you can see it – then you can be sure your route is clearly marked and there will be no difficulty if you have to retrace your steps.

OTHER METHODS OF ROUTE MARKING

If you have no means of blazing trees, or you wish to mark your route in an area where there are no trees, you must use other methods. The main thing is that the signs you make should be different from their surroundings, so:

1. Build small, regular piles of stones (cairns). These are particularly useful on open, rocky ridges.

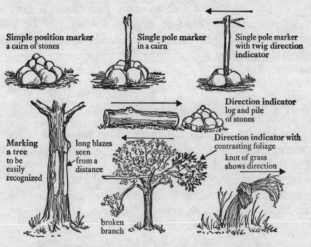

Simple position marker
a cairn of stones

Single pole marker
in a cairn

Single pole marker
with twig **direction**
indicator

Direction indicator
log and pile
of stones

**Marking
a tree
to be
easily
recognized**

long blazes
seen
from a
distance

Direction indicator with
contrasting foliage

knot of grass
shows direction

broken
branch

Fig. 37 Position markers and direction indicators

2. Break the ends of tree or shrub branches so they hang down, and if possible push a different kind of leafy branch through the broken portion.
3. Push a thin pole into the ground. Split the top of the pole and insert a twig or leaf pointing in the direction of travel.

4. Tie tall grass into a knot with the free end indicating direction.
5. Arrange small logs or branches to indicate line of travel and place stones or leaves at one end as an 'arrowhead'.

TRAVELLING ON FOREST RIDGES

Whenever you are unsure of the direction you should take when travelling on a ridge in forest areas **mark the spot to which you consider you may need to return.**

Make sure that it is obvious from every direction. Four long blazes on each quarter of a tree; a large cone-shaped pile of timber; stones with a central pole of wood. Any of these position markers (see diagram above) may be used with a direction indicator, and they can be seen from a considerable distance.

MAPS AND MAP READING

If you have a topographical * map which you know includes the area in which you are a survivor – then you have a very important survival aid.

If you have a **contour map**, the information you can gain from it is considerable. Contour lines are lines which are drawn on a map to indicate the shape (contour) of the land mass at any particular height.

It is easy to visualize how contour lines give you a 'picture' of the land if you think of them as *water-level lines*. Simply imagine a mountain, any mountain, with its ridges and valleys, steep rock faces and gentle slopes. Then imagine that the sea invades the land and starts to rise up the mountain. The water would flow round ridges and enter

* 'Topographical' means 'the detailed description of natural land features, and their representations by symbols'.

the valleys, and if a line was drawn all round the water's edge at any particular moment, that would be a *contour line*. If a series of such lines was drawn at intervals as the sea rose, say every hundred metres, and then after all the land had been covered the sea was drained away – there would be a series of lines, each one separated vertically from the next by 100 metres. If your imagination is still equal to the task, imagine that a photograph is now taken looking down directly on to the mountain. The resulting picture would show the mountain in a flat, two-dimensional form – but it would be covered in contour lines, and these lines would show by their shape the actual vertical form of the mountain.

READING A CONTOUR MAP

The diagram which follows shows a method you can use to obtain a cross-sectioned profile from a contour map. Part of a typical contour map is shown, with a valley running diagonally from the south-west to the middle of the map where it divides and branches to the NW., NE. and SE. To the west of the valley there is a mountain 500 metres high, and to the south another mountain 510 metres.

The heavy black line (A–B) on the map has been drawn from the top of the mountain to the west through the top of the mountain to the south in order to plot the profile between these two points. It could, of course, have been drawn anywhere and any length on the map, depending on what information was required.

Beneath the map, a series of horizontal, regularly spaced parallel lines have been drawn, and these lines have been labelled with heights, starting from the bottom with the lowest contour line height that the heavy black line crosses (430 m) and ending with the highest (510 m).

Now it is only necessary to draw lines to these height

lines from where each contour line of a particular height is cut by the heavy black line (A–B). The ends of these lines on the height chart are now joined with a continuous line, and the profile (C–D) is revealed.

If you look at the profile line you will see that the slope

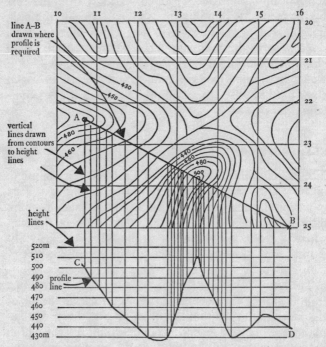

Fig. 38 Plotting a profile line between two points on a contour map

down to the valley from the west is much less steep than the slope leading up to the mountain top to the east: the corresponding contour lines of the western slope are farther apart than those on the eastern slope, so the farther apart the contour lines **the less the slope,** and the closer together they are **the greater the slope.**

Further points to note:

1. Contour lines which are close together at the top of a hill and are farther apart lower down show that the **slope is concave** and the bottom of the slope will be visible from the top.
2. Contour lines which are close together at the bottom of a hill and are farther apart towards the top show that the **slope is convex.**
3. Contour lines on ridges point downhill, and in valleys, upstream.

HACHURES

On some maps the varying degree of steepness of slopes is shown by means of a system known as hachuring. Hachures consist of a series of short lines, thick and close together to indicate steep slopes, thin and farther apart for more gentle slopes. It is not possible to give completely accurate height

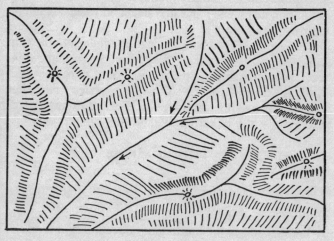

Fig. 39 Hachures on a map show steep or gentle slopes

information or shape of slopes with hachuring, but it does indicate the general form of land masses.

OTHER INFORMATION ON MAPS

Topographical maps give you a large amount of information which enables you to:

1. Build up a mental picture of the land portrayed.
2. Measure distances.
3. Plan routes.
4. Give your position.

Legend

At the foot of your map you will generally find a comprehensive 'legend' – a series of symbols for all the different natural and man-made features which are in the area covered by the map. Man-made features shown on maps are not always reliable indications that they actually exist – sometimes roads which have been surveyed but never made are put on maps, and roads may be found which are not on your map.

Reading the legend and relating the symbols to the map can save you from making serious time-consuming mistakes. A good example is the importance of recognizing the symbols for swampy areas. These are perfectly flat, but travelling through such areas – if they are of any appreciable size – may be extremely difficult, or impossible.

ALIGNING A MAP WITH THE LANDSCAPE IT REPRESENTS

There are two main methods you can use to align (orient) a topographical map with the features it represents.

1. You can line up the north–south direction shown on the map with the earth's actual north–south direction. This

requires a magnetic compass, or some way of locating the north–south line. **OR:**

2. If you can recognize ground features (three, if possible) which correspond with features shown on the map, then by turning the map you can place it in the position where the ground features 'fit' the map.

USING A MAGNETIC COMPASS

A magnetic compass is a *direction-indicating device* which consists of a magnetized needle mounted on a pivot. If allowed to swing freely in any direction, the needle will

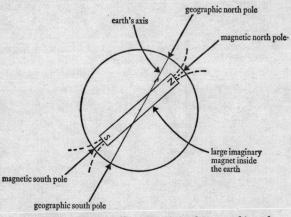

Fig. 40 The earth's magnetic and geographic poles

come to rest pointing towards the earth's **magnetic north** and not the earth's **true geographic north**. This is due to the fact that the north and south geographic poles do not coincide with the north and south magnetic poles. This is easily understood if the earth is thought of as containing a giant magnet which is at an angle to the line through the earth's north and south geographic poles.

Magnetic Declination or Variation

Since the needle of a magnetic compass points to the magnetic north and not to the true north, it is necessary to know the angular difference between these two directions if accurate orientation of a map with the corresponding ground features is to be made (or **true bearings** (see page 102) are to be calculated).

Depending on where you are in the world, this *angular difference* is east or west of true north and is called the **magnetic declination**. It is often shown on maps in the form of a diagram.

magnetic declination
1970
23° 40′
annual variation
+9.2′

Fig. 41 Method on some maps of showing true north and magnetic north

The year the magnetic declination was measured is generally shown, together with the amount it varies annually in minutes, and fractions of a minute. This annual variation is due to the continuous movement of the magnetic north and south poles. The magnetic declination is often called the **variation**.

Calculating the Total Variation

To calculate the total variation, which enables you to orient your map correctly, proceed as follows:

(a) Note the magnetic declination in degrees and minutes as shown on the map.

(b) Note the year the measurement was made.

(c) Note the annual variation and whether it is plus (+) or minus (−).

1. Multiply the number of years since the map was made by the annual variation.

2. Add the answer to this calculation to the magnetic declination if it is plus (+); subtract the answer if it is minus (−). The sum obtained by the addition or subtraction of these figures is the total variation.

For example:

(a) Magnetic declination: 20° 40′ **east**

(b) Year of measurement: 1960

(c) Annual variation: +9′.4

1. Number of years since the map was made = 15, so the calculation becomes 15 × 9′.4 = 141′.0, and this divided by 60 (since there are 60 minutes in a degree) becomes 2° 21′.

2. Add 2° 21′ to the magnetic declination (20° 40′) and the total variation is 23° 1′.

Direction Given as a Compass Bearing

A direction of travel can be stated in *degrees* starting with north as 0° (zero degrees) and going clockwise round the circle to 360°, which brings you back to north. The number of degrees is a compass **bearing**.

An easy way to understand this method of giving direction is to imagine that you are standing at the centre of

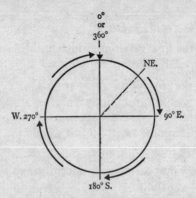

Fig. 42 Compass bearings given in degrees and read in clockwise direction

a large compass and there are lines radiating out from you through the various degree positions.

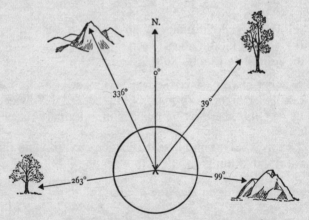

Fig. 43 Compass bearings radiating out from an observer

Magnetic Bearings and True Bearings

Bearings can be either *magnetic* or *true*. Magnetic bearings are bearings expressed in degrees from magnetic north, taking magnetic north as 0°. *True* bearings are expressed in degrees from true north, taking true north as 0°. To convert a magnetic bearing to a true bearing simply **add** or **subtract** the variation to the magnetic bearing, depending on whether the variation is plus or minus. Example: magnetic bearing 50° and a variation of +11°E = 61° true.

When giving bearings, always state if magnetic or true.

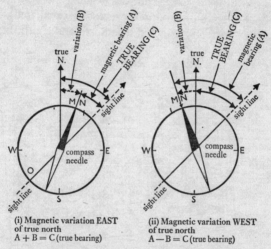

(i) Magnetic variation EAST of true north
A + B = C (true bearing)

(ii) Magnetic variation WEST of true north
A − B = C (true bearing)

Fig. 44 Converting magnetic bearings to true bearings

ALIGNING A MAP TRUE NORTH AND SOUTH

On the majority of topographical maps a system of horizontal and vertical *grid lines* are used to divide the map into squares. (Depending on the country of origin of the map, and when it was drawn, the length represented by the sides of these squares may be 1,000 yards or 1,000 metres.)

The vertical lines making up the grid are generally arranged to lie almost in the true north–south direction, and to orient your map correctly it is necessary to ensure that these lines are aligned with the true north–south direction.

You should spread the map out flat on the ground, making sure there are no iron or steel objects under it or near it. Place the compass on the map so that the north–south line of the compass is over one of the vertical grid lines, or over a true north line if one is provided at the bottom of the map, or in the margin. Now turn the map and compass together until the compass needle is pointing to the number of degrees of variation (previously calculated). The map is then correctly oriented true north and south.

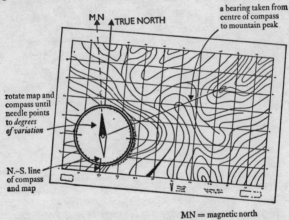

MN = magnetic north

Fig. 45 Aligning a map true north and south and taking a bearing

TAKING A COMPASS BEARING AND STEERING A COMPASS COURSE

The type of compass you have will determine the procedure you use to take bearings or to steer a compass course. If you have a precision instrument complete with sighting device and movable bearing ring, then you should proceed as shown for **precision compass**. If you have a very simple compass, even of the 'cracker' variety, follow the procedure shown under **simple compass**.

Precision Compass

Taking a bearing: Since the compass needle points to the magnetic north, you will find it easier to take magnetic bearings than true bearings. Magnetic bearings are perfectly satisfactory for your own cross-country travelling purposes, and you only need to convert them to true bearings if you are working from the **true north–south lines** on the map.

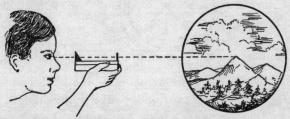

Fig. 46 Taking a compass bearing

Procedure: If your compass has a lock to hold the needle steady when not in use, you should first make sure it is released. (Generally, there is a small lever or button on the side of the compass, or sometimes, opening the compass releases the lock.)

Hold the compass level with your eye, as shown in Fig. 46, and line up the sights with the object on which you are taking the bearing. When the needle is at rest, rotate the *bearing ring* (see Fig. 47, page 106) until the north-seeking end of the needle (it will probably be marked) is pointing at the zero degree (0°), or north mark.

The required bearing will now be indicated by the 'lubber line', which is the fixed mark on your compass in line with the sighting line.

Steering a compass course with a precision compass:
Using your compass to steer in a particular direction involves finding the bearing of the direction in which you wish to proceed and then setting this bearing on the compass. The bearing may be found from the map, particularly if you are in a heavily forested area, or it may be found as

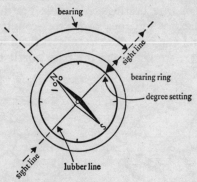

Fig. 47 Taking a compass bearing with a precision compass

described above. (If you want to find a bearing from the map, you must first know your position. If you know this with reasonable accuracy, align the map north and south, and place the centre of the compass over your position. Read off a bearing as shown in Fig. 47.)

To proceed along the bearing direction, locate some object along the sight-line which can be kept in sight while you proceed towards it. Since the object you choose will be along the required bearing line, you only need to proceed towards it and you will be travelling in the right direction. When you reach the object, take a new sighting with the compass and select a new object. In open country, or in a mountainous area, the object you select may be a considerable distance away, so that repeated sightings may not be necessary. It is more difficult to maintain an accurate bearing direction in a forested area, and the number of sightings you make will need to be more numerous, since the object you choose to steer towards will most probably be a tree or bush, and your line of sight will be much shorter.

Simple Compass

Taking a bearing: This technique is the complete reverse of the procedure described for taking a bearing with a precision compass.

Hold the compass so that you can sight across it, and turn it until the north–south line of the compass is lined up with the object whose bearing is required. When the needle comes to rest, read off its position in degrees. (If the compass is not graduated in degrees the bearing will not be accurate, but you can still steer a compass course with it.)

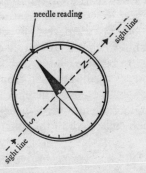

Fig. 48 Taking a compass bearing with a simple compass

A reading in degrees obtained by this method may be converted to a magnetic bearing by subtracting it from 360°. For example, if the reading is 280°, then the bearing is 360° − 280° = 80° magnetic.

Steering a compass course with a simple compass: use the compass in the same way as described for taking a bearing – north point of compass pointing in the required direction, and the reading or position of the needle noted when it comes to rest.

Walk towards some object in the required direction, and when it is reached, hold the compass once again with the needle indicating the previous reading. Continue in the direction indicated by the north–south line of the compass.

ALIGNING A MAP WITHOUT A COMPASS

If you have a map but lack a compass there are several alternatives open to you which enable a north–south line to be located, or the map to be aligned.

Regardless of the method you choose, there is one important point which must be kept before your mind at all times – **the sun rises in the east and sets in the west,** and the **stars** appear to move from **east** to **west** also.

Such information may seem very obvious and ordinary 'common sense', but when you are in a shocked or confused state it is also easy to become confused about such a simple thing. Also, if you are used to the sun rising to your south, if you live in the northern hemisphere, or to your north if you live in the southern hemisphere, then a change in your location from one hemisphere to the other can prove confusing also.

Finding the North–South Meridian

A line on the earth's surface which, if extended, would pass through the north and south geographic poles is called the north–south meridian line. If an accurate north–south meridian line can be found, then the aligning of a map without a compass is simple. All that is necessary is to line up the **true** north–south lines on the map with the meridian line.

Methods

1. **Using a watch to find the meridian**: This method is **not** accurate or reliable, except on the following occasions: sunrise and sunset on 21 March and 23 September, and at any place at noon, if you are sure that your watch is on accurate local time. Provided you realize the results are an approximation only, the method is as follows: Hold the watch horizontal and point the hour hand at the sun. A line half-way between the hour hand and twelve is taken as south if you are in the northern hemisphere and north if you are in the southern hemisphere.

   Do not rely on this method; it is subject to serious inaccuracies.

2. **Finding the north–south meridian by the shadow-stick method**: this method gives a very accurate *north–south meridian*. It requires a few hours of time and a fine day, with uninterrupted sunshine for at least two hours, but the only 'equipment' required is a stake approximately two thirds of a metre in length, some short sticks of a few centimetres to use as marking pegs, and a piece of cord or string. (If necessary, since it is only for temporary use, you can use your belt, or shoelace. Lacking either, use a forked stick, as shown in the diagram.)

   (a) Clear some flat ground where the sun will shine for at least two hours or more. Push the stake vertically into the ground and mark the end of the shadow cast by it with a short peg. Describe a circle on the ground, using the length of the shadow from the stake as the radius.

      At intervals of 10–15 minutes (or, if you do not have a watch, whenever the shadow has obviously moved), mark the position of the end of the shadow with a peg. When you have recorded several positions over a period of 2–3 hours, scratch a line on the ground to join all the positions of the pegs into a smooth curve. Continue the curve until it meets the circle previously drawn. (The curve will be either concave or convex.)

(b) Join the two points on either side of the circle where the curve intercepts it, and you have a **true east–west line**. If a line is now drawn from the stake through the mid-point of this east–west line, it will be the **true north–south meridian**.

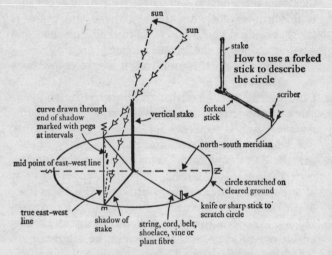

Fig. 49 Finding the north–south meridian line

There are two periods during the year when the points marked on the shadow moves are in an exact line east and west. This occurs during the two equinoxes (when the sun is directly over the equator) on 21 March and 21 September, and since there is not a great amount of north or south movement of the sun around these dates you can accept that the line traced by the shadow is near enough to **east–west** for practical purposes from approximately 7 March to 7 April, and from 7 September to 7 October.

Finding North or South from the Stars
Northern Hemisphere

Location of **true north** from the stars in the northern hemisphere is simplified by the fact that **Polaris**, the **Pole Star**, is almost directly over the North Pole, as can be seen from the star chart.

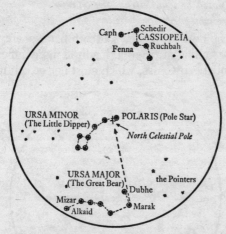

Fig. 50 Star chart : northern polar region

The two pointers of the *Big Dipper* (*Dubhe* and *Merak*) point roughly towards the North Pole, and the distance from midway between these two stars is two 'thumb and middle finger spans', or 30°.

The constellation of *Cassiopeia* has the appearance of a 'W' and the star in the top middle position (*Fenna*) also points towards the North Pole. Once again, the distance is two 'thumb and middle finger spans' (30°).

Two 'thumb and middle finger spans' from *Ruchbah* in *Cassiopeia* taken towards *Mizar* in the handle of the *Big Dipper* also gives the **Pole Star** position.

Finding the *eastern or western horizon* is not difficult if the weather is clear, if you look for where stars are suddenly appearing (east) and sinking out of sight (west).

South can also be found by looking for stars which are low down in the sky towards the horizon, and which appear to be moving on a short, flat path. The central point where this movement is apparent is **true south**.

Finding North or South from the Stars
Southern Hemisphere

There is no pole star in the southern hemisphere, and this makes the finding of true south a little more difficult.

The **Southern Cross**, which must not be confused with

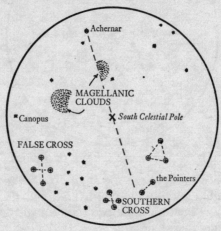

Fig. 51 Star chart: southern polar region

the False Cross, is one of the best groups of stars to use for finding south, since it is visible anywhere in the southern hemisphere, and as far north as 25° north of the equator.

Near the *True Cross* are two bright stars, the *Pointers*, and these help you to identify the Cross accurately. Two 'thumb and middle finger spans' from a position near the *Pointer* nearest to the *Cross*, taken in the direction of

Achernar, gives you the position of the **true South Pole**.

The long axis of the *Cross* (head-to-tail line) points almost to the South Pole. If the Cross is extended $4\frac{1}{2}$ times its length, measured from its base, you will find a point in the sky which is close to being directly over the pole.

If the stars *Achernar* and *Canopus* are visible, then another method you can use is to imagine that a line joining these two stars is the base of a triangle, with sides of the same length. The apex of this triangle lies over the South Pole.

Similarly, if the mid-point of the *Magellanic Clouds* is taken as the base of a triangle with sides of equal length, the apex of the triangle is once again over the South Pole.

In a similar manner to the way stars in the south are seen moving in flat paths near the horizon when viewed from the north, the northern stars are seen moving in flat paths when viewed from the south.

Equatorial Regions

If you are near the equator, one of the best indications of **east** and **west**, and thus indirectly north and south, is that stars rising due east **rise vertically**, pass overhead and **sink vertically** down below the western horizon.

If you are right on the equator, stars which rise due east of you will also pass directly overhead.

If the constellation *Orion's Belt* is visible, a line drawn through the stars *Saiph* and *Betelgeux* gives an approximate north–south line.

Whether you live in the northern or southern hemisphere it pays to be able to recognize the stars and constellations necessary for locating north or south. Use every available clear night you can to study the stars.

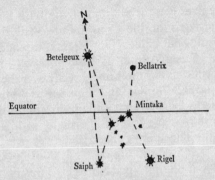

Fig. 52 Finding approximate north direction from Orion

ORIENTATION OF THE MAP

When you have located the north–south meridian, or the direction of the North or South Pole, a line scratched on the ground will assist you to line up the north–south line of your map. If there are no north–south grid lines, or other indications of north on the map, the top should be taken as north, since most maps are drawn in this way.

Orientation from Ground Features

If you can recognize prominent physical features of the landscape and identify them on a map, you have a somewhat rough method of map orientation. All that is necessary, having identified some ground features which correspond with those on the map, is to turn it until the same features on the map are in the same positions as the land features. If several ground features can be found which are undeniably those you can locate on the map, then the error obtained by lining up the map in this way can be kept to a minimum. (See Fig. 53 opposite.)

line of sight
to actual ground
feature
corresponding
to map position

Fig. 53 Orientation of map by ground features

GIVING A MAP REFERENCE

The majority of topographical maps have a numbered
system of grid-lines which enable you to inform someone else (who may be hundreds, or even thousands of
kilometres away) **precisely where you are**. Figure 54
shows a small section of a map with its grid-lines. These
lines form a square which encloses a stream junction (X).
The horizontal grid-lines for this particular square are
numbered 22 and 23 (numbered from north to south),
while the vertical grid-lines are numbered 13 and 14 (numbered from west to east). Grid squares generally have sides
with a length of 1,000 yards, or 1,000 metres, and by
dividing the sides into ten parts it is possible to state how
many *tenths* of the length a particular position is from the
west side of a square, or from the south side.

Calculating a Reference

To fix the position of the stream junction, and *to express it in* numbers, the method is as follows:

The vertical line on the *western side* of the square is taken *first* and its number written down – in this case, it is 13. Then the number of tenths eastwards that the stream junction lies from this line is estimated – in this case, 7. Thus the first three numbers of the position reference is 137.

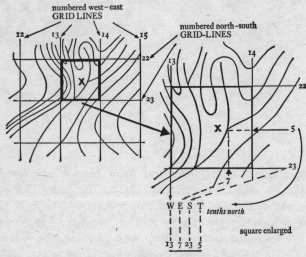

Fig. 54 How to give a map reference

Next, the horizontal line on the *southern side* of the square is taken – in this case, it is numbered 23, so this is written next to give a five-figure number: 13723. It is now only necessary to estimate the tenths northwards of the stream junction – in this case, 5, and write it as the final figure of the reference.

The complete reference figure is 137235, and this fixes the position of the stream junction.

Name the Map

If you give a map reference of your position there is one other important piece of information you must give – the name of the area the map covers, or its number, if it has one.

How to remember the map reference system: remember the word 'west'. You can see from the diagram how it helps you to remember the method of giving a map reference:

W = the *west* side of the square – give its number
E = the number of tenths *east* from the west line
S = the *south* side of the square – give its number
T = tenths *north* from the south side of the square.

LOST

To be 'lost' is one of the more unenviable situations that you, as a survivor, may find yourself in, and if, through some disaster, *you have no knowledge of your location at all*, then all your efforts must go towards maintaining yourself until rescued.

LOSS OF DIRECTION

Loss of direction is somewhat different from being lost, since there is quite often a considerable amount that you can do to remedy the situation. There is one simple rule, however, which applies to 'being lost', and which must be followed. *If you lose your bearings; if you are suddenly separated from all other human contacts; if you are confused about your whereabouts* **stop and sit down**. This one simple action helps prevent PANIC and helps to clear your mind and allow for a calm appraisal of your situation.

It is worth repeating this rule so that it is fixed in your mind – if you ever think that you are lost, and a sinking feeling in the pit of your stomach tells you that you are completely on your own without the vaguest idea which way you should go –

Stop and sit down.

With your mind calm and relaxed you are ready for action, and the time of the day will largely determine what your actions should be.

If it is late in the day, then you must consider the fact that you may have to stay where you are so that you can start fresh in the morning.

If there is plenty of daylight time left, you may decide that by moving in a particular direction you can re-establish your whereabouts. Before you move off anywhere, however, **mark your position** (see page 93) and make sure that the spot will be clearly recognizable whatever means you use, and regardless of the direction you approach it from.

MAKING A SKETCH MAP

When you have lost your direction and are not sure which way to proceed, there is always a particular time in the past when you did know where you were. To attempt to establish where this point was and to return to it you can make a sketch with no equipment whatever, except a stick and some bare ground to draw on. Clear an area on the ground so that you have bare earth, if possible, and then, with a stick, start marking in all the features you can remember until a map is built up. Draw lines for ridges or streams crossed or followed, and you may be surprised to find that it wasn't as long ago as you thought it was that you actually knew where you were. Even if the sketch map does not seem to be of much assistance, make sure you *mark your position* before making your next move.

If you can recall crossing a stream, then you may be able to back-track to it and eventually follow it, since it will most probably lead into a larger waterway system. Also, a stream provides water for you, if and when you decide to establish a camp.

GENERAL RULE OF TRAVEL WHEN LOST

Although you should follow a stream with caution, and to do so is not always recommended, it is a procedure which should be adopted if you have lost your way and no amount of thought and observation appears to be of any assistance. Streams invariably lead into larger waterways and rivers, and these ultimately make their way, in the majority of cases, out to inhabited or farmed land.

A SEARCH TECHNIQUE FOR FINDING A LOST TRACK, TRAIL OR PATHWAY

The explorer Francis Galton developed an interesting technique to enable a lost track, trail or pathway to be found, provided you are equipped with a compass. If you have been following a clearly-defined pathway and then discover that somehow you have wandered off it and it is no longer visible, it would be possible to find it by travelling in a circle with its centre established where you first lost your way, and with a radius chosen so that it would undoubtedly intercept the pathway at some point.

The difficulty with this idea, however, is that to follow a circular path – particularly in a forested area – is almost impossible. To overcome this, Galton devised the method which is shown in the diagram, and provided you do not make the sides of the figure too short when you come to pace it out, then it is a most effective 'trail finder'.

The method is as follows:

Having decided that you are no longer certain which way you should proceed, you must ask yourself this question – how long is it since I was certain about the path I was following?

The answer to this question will tell you how far you will need to travel in your search to regain the path.

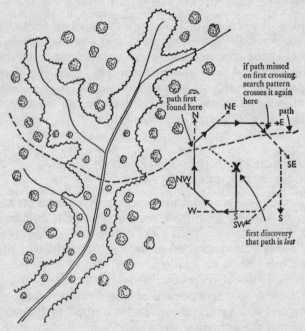

Fig. 55 A search technique for finding a lost path

The diagram shows the 'search pattern' which you must follow, and a compass is absolutely essential – since each 'leg' of the search pattern is along a definite bearing.

15 Minutes or Less

If it is *15 minutes or less* since you were certain of your path, the baseline distance on which your search pattern should be based is 120 paces.

Over 15 Minutes

If it is *more than 15 minutes* since you were certain of your path, the baseline distance on which your search pattern should be based is 200 paces.

Note: If you are not successful with either of these two distances, it is better to repeat the search pattern from other points, rather than to increase the number of paces. The reason for this is that with 120 paces as your baseline, the maximum distance you will travel is about $\frac{7}{10}$ of a kilometre, while with 200 paces you cover a maximum distance of $1\frac{1}{5}$ kilometres – just looking for your lost path. Increasing the number of paces not only increases the distance, it also increases the time required.

Setting Off to Search

Having decided what your baseline distance is to be, do not move until you have marked your position. The diagram shows this point with an X. From this point you take a bearing with your compass of 180° magnetic (due south), and pace your chosen distance of 120 or 200 paces. You then take a bearing of 270° magnetic (due west) and pace out a distance of $\frac{2}{5}$ of your baseline (48 paces if your first distance was 120 paces, or 80 paces if your first distance was 200 paces).

You then take a bearing of 315° (NW.) and pace out $\frac{4}{5}$

of your distance (96 if 120 paces, 160 if 200 paces). Now
take a bearing of 360° (N.) and pace out 96 or 160 paces
again. Next, take a bearing of 45° (NE.) and pace 96 or 160
paces. Follow this with a bearing of 90° (E.) and 96 or 160
paces, then a bearing of 135° (SE.) and 96 or 160 paces,
then 180° (S.) and 96 or 160 paces, then 225° (SW.) and 96
or 160 paces, and finally 270° (W.) and $\frac{2}{5}$ of your first distance, again 48 or 80 paces. For convenience, these bearings
and distances are set out in the following chart:

Search 'Leg'	Bearing (magnetic)	Number of paces to take	
		Baseline 120 paces	*Baseline* 200 paces
		Start	Start
1	180° (S.)	120	200
2	270° (W.)	48	80
3	315° (NW.)	96	160
4	360° (N.)	96	160
5	45° (NE.)	96	160
6	90° (E.)	96	160
7	135° (SE.)	96	160
8	180° (S.)	96	160
9	225° (SW.)	96	160
10	270° (W.)	48	80
		Finish	Finish

Before carrying out this search system, it is advisable to
scratch a diagram on the ground so that there is no confusion in your mind about the route to be followed.

TRAPS AND TRAPPING

Construction of traps and snares from natural materials takes time and effort, but the results obtained can be rewarding if some simple principles are followed:

1. Set traps and snares where signs of animals or birds are seen – tracks, droppings, browsed foliage, gnawed bark, claw scratches on trees, fruit remains. It is a waste of time to construct a perfect trap if it is not situated where there are animals or birds for it to catch.
2. A trap must be constructed for the particular animal it is intended to capture – a trap for rabbits is of no use if the only animals in the area are deer. Also, traps which are too light in construction for their intended catch may be sprung without result. Time spent making a strong trap is never time wasted.
3. Animals are warned of danger by their noses, rather than by their eyes. Your traps and snares are much more likely to succeed if you pay attention to removing your human scent, rather than trying to disguise them to look 'natural'. Fire is an effective scent remover, and passing parts of a trap through the flames of a small fire acts as a deodorant. A trap left out in the weather for a considerable period also loses its human scent, but since you probably cannot wait that long, dowsing the trap with water after it has been constructed achieves much the same effect.

The diagrams which follow are all self-explanatory – note that fishing methods are also included under 'traps'.

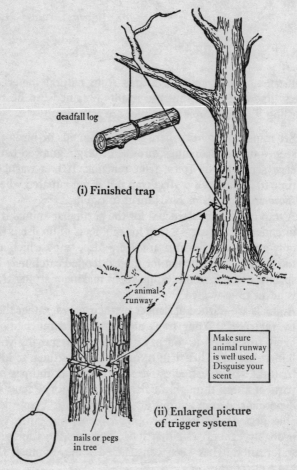

deadfall log

(i) Finished trap

animal runway

Make sure
animal runway
is well used.
Disguise your
scent

**(ii) Enlarged picture
of trigger system**

nails or pegs
in tree

Fig. 56 Snare trap with deadfall for ground animals and birds

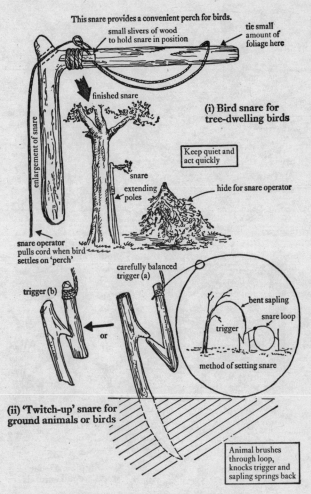

This snare provides a convenient perch for birds.

small slivers of wood to hold snare in position

tie small amount of foliage here

finished snare

enlargement of snare

(i) Bird snare for tree-dwelling birds

Keep quiet and act quickly

snare

extending poles

hide for snare operator

snare operator pulls cord when bird settles on 'perch'

carefully balanced trigger (a)

trigger (b)

or

bent sapling

snare loop

trigger

method of setting snare

(ii) 'Twitch-up' snare for ground animals or birds

Animal brushes through loop, knocks trigger and sapling springs back

Fig. 57 Bird snare and 'twitch-up' snare

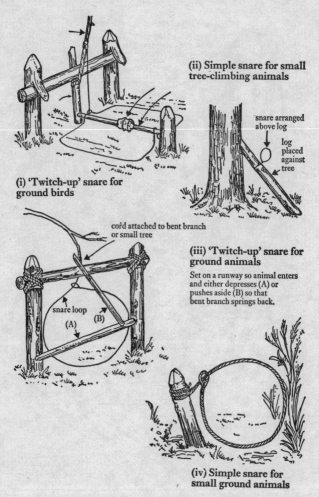

(ii) Simple snare for small tree-climbing animals

snare arranged above log

log placed against tree

(i) 'Twitch-up' snare for ground birds

cord attached to bent branch or small tree

(iii) 'Twitch-up' snare for ground animals

Set on a runway so animal enters and either depresses (A) or pushes aside (B) so that bent branch springs back.

snare loop

(A)   (B)

(iv) Simple snare for small ground animals

Fig. 58 Snares for small animals and birds

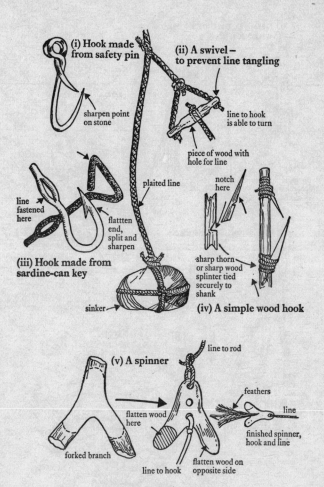

(i) Hook made from safety pin

sharpen point on stone

(ii) A swivel – to prevent line tangling

line to hook is able to turn

piece of wood with hole for line

plaited line

line fastened here

flattten end, split and sharpen

(iii) Hook made from sardine-can key

sinker

notch here

sharp thorn or sharp wood splinter tied securely to shank

(iv) A simple wood hook

(v) A spinner

line to rod

feathers

line

flatten wood here

finished spinner, hook and line

forked branch

line to hook

flatten wood on opposite side

Fig. 59 Fishing equipment

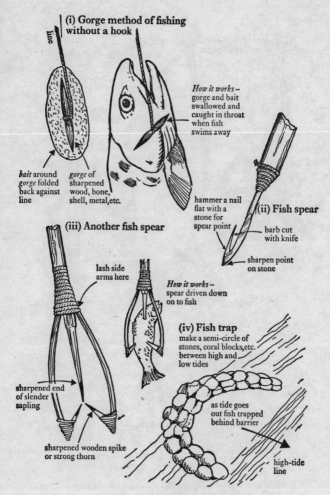

(i) Gorge method of fishing without a hook

line

How it works — gorge and bait swallowed and caught in throat when fish swims away

bait around **gorge** folded back against line

gorge of sharpened wood, bone, shell, metal, etc.

hammer a nail flat with a stone for spear point

(ii) Fish spear

barb cut with knife

sharpen point on stone

(iii) Another fish spear

lash side arms here

How it works — spear driven down on to fish

(iv) Fish trap make a semi-circle of stones, coral blocks, etc. between high and low tides

sharpened end of slender sapling

as tide goes out fish trapped behind barrier

sharpened wooden spike or strong thorn

high-tide line

Fig. 60 More fishing equipment

HUNTING

If food is very short and your traps and snares are not providing you with any food, you may have to try hunting small animals. Here are some hints on how to hunt successfully – and *safely*. Remember it is a dangerous thing to do and you should be very careful and only attempt hunting when you have no other means of getting food. Approach *any* animal with great care and caution – it may be frightened and on the defensive, so be ready to defend yourself until you know the animal is dead. (Test to see if an animal is dead by touching its eyeball with your finger – if the eye blinks, the animal is not dead.)

1. SEARCH FOR SIGN

'Sign' is anything which indicates that game is present and that hunting and setting traps is worth the effort. If you see obvious trails or runways; footprints in soft ground; droppings (if these are warm or shiny, the animal is not far away); browsed foliage or chewed leaves; trampled ground near a water-hole or stream – any or all of these signs are indications that hunting is worthwhile. Once you have found what appears to be a well-used trail, you should take care not to disturb it too much. It is better to keep away from it but at the same time look for a position which will enable you to keep it under surveillance. Any trail which leads to water, a forest clearing, or out on to open grasslands is worth considering. Get yourself into a hiding place in the early morning, or late in the afternoon, so that you can see any game coming to or going from water or food.

2. ALLOW FOR ANIMAL SENSES

The sense of smell is highly developed in most game animals, since their survival depends on quickly becoming aware of danger. They respond to the warning received by their noses far more quickly than by what they see.

Unless you approach an animal with the wind (even a breeze) blowing *from it* towards you (downwind), it is doubtful if you will get very close before it flees. In fact, your scent may so effectively advertise your presence that you may not even see an animal which has moved quietly away.

To test for wind or breeze direction, you can toss any light material into the air (dust, dry grass, feathers) and see which way it moves. Or you can use the time-honoured method of wetting your finger in your mouth and then holding it up – it will feel coldest on the side the wind is coming from.

If the wind direction is unfavourable when you first sight game, it is best to make your way in a wide circle around the quarry until you are in a better position to move forward.

3. AVOID UNDUE SOUND AND MOVEMENT

Grazing animals raise their heads suddenly at varying intervals and any movement they may see which arouses their suspicion is likely to cause flight. Should you be stalking an animal through limited cover, or over open ground, and it should look towards you – **stand absolutely still.** Once satisfied that there is no danger it may resume feeding.

If you are stalking on a mountain or hill face, try to get yourself into a position above your quarry. Animals tend to look for danger coming from below, and your chances of success are increased considerably if you can make your approach from the upper slopes, but avoid silhouetting yourself against the skyline.

It is not always easy to move through forest without any sound and if there is thick undergrowth then you must take care not to allow branches to spring back if you push them aside. Place your feet firmly without breaking sticks or kicking stones so that you do not make any noise.

MORE AIDS FOR SURVIVAL

The diagrams that follow show how to make more aids out of natural materials. The raft (page 132) in particular requires a great deal of time, effort and materials; before you attempt making this and any of the other tools, make sure you have plenty of these three 'commodities'.

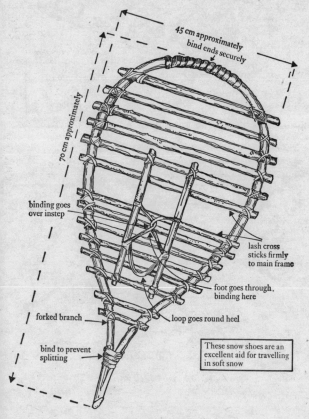

45 cm approximately
bind ends securely

70 cm approximately

binding goes
over instep

lash cross
sticks firmly
to main frame

foot goes through
binding here

forked branch

loop goes round heel

bind to prevent
splitting

These snow shoes are an
excellent aid for travelling
in soft snow

Fig. 61 A sapling snow shoe

(i) The finished raft

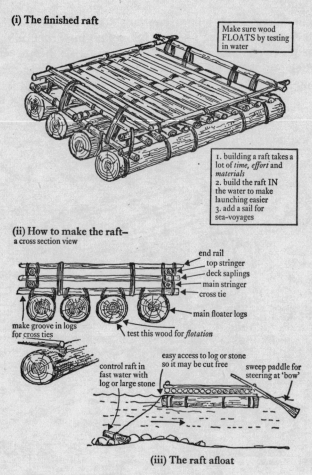

Make sure wood FLOATS by testing in water

1. building a raft takes a lot of *time*, *effort* and *materials*
2. build the raft IN the water to make launching easier
3. add a sail for sea-voyages

(ii) How to make the raft—
a cross section view

end rail
top stringer
deck saplings
main stringer
cross tie

main floater logs

make groove in logs for cross ties

test this wood for *flotation*

easy access to log or stone so it may be cut free

control raft in fast water with log or large stone

sweep paddle for steering at 'bow'

(iii) The raft afloat

Fig. 62 A wooden raft

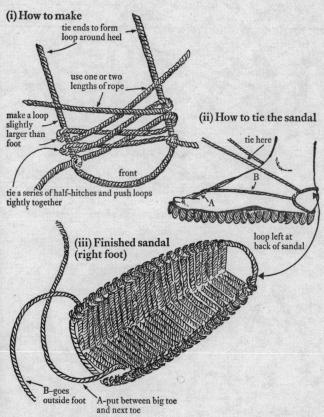

(i) How to make

tie ends to form
loop around heel

use one or two
lengths of rope

make a loop
slightly
larger than
foot

(ii) How to tie the sandal

tie here

B

A

front

tie a series of half-hitches and push loops
tightly together

loop left at
back of sandal

**(iii) Finished sandal
(right foot)**

B–goes
outside foot

A–put between big toe
and next toe

Fig. 63 Sandals made from length of rope or twisted plant fibres

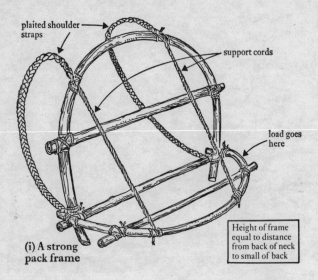

plaited shoulder straps

support cords

load goes here

(i) A strong pack frame

Height of frame equal to distance from back of neck to small of back

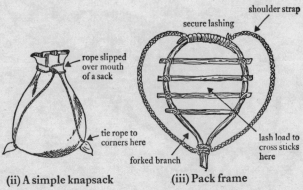

shoulder strap

secure lashing

rope slipped over mouth of a sack

tie rope to corners here

forked branch

lash load to cross sticks here

(ii) A simple knapsack

(iii) Pack frame

Fig. 64 Pack frames and a knapsack made from a sack

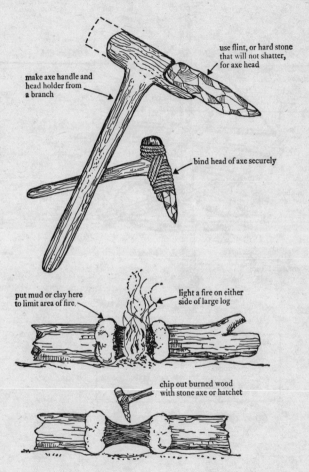

use flint, or hard stone that will not shatter, for axe head

make axe handle and head holder from a branch

bind head of axe securely

put mud or clay here to limit area of fire

light a fire on either side of large log

chip out burned wood with stone axe or hatchet

Fig. 65 Making a stone axe and 'cutting' a large log

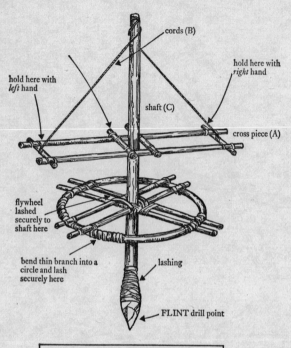

cords (B)

hold here with
right hand

hold here with
left hand

shaft (C)

cross piece (A)

flywheel
lashed
securely to
shaft here

bend thin branch into a
circle and lash
securely here

lashing

FLINT drill point

How it works
1. cross piece (A) is pushed down by both hands
2. cords (B) which are wound round drill shaft (C) cause it to rotate
3. shaft rotating causes cords to wind in the opposite direction *and*
4. cross piece is lifted again

Fig. 66 A drill to bore holes in wood, shell or soft stone

6. Water

'W' stands for water in the survival formula, and it has been deliberately arranged to come before 'F' for food – the last word in the formula, and the last chapter in the book. The reason for this is simple – you can live for a considerable time, several weeks in fact, without food, but without water your chances of survival are reduced to days – and the higher the temperature the fewer the days.

Approximately three fifths (60 per cent) of the human body is composed of water and the diagram shows the

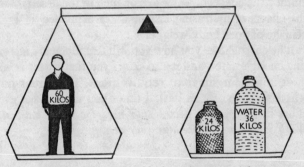

Fig. 67 The ratio of body and water weight

quantity of water present in a person weighing 60 kilograms. The amount of water (36 kg) appears to be considerable, but the loss of even small quantities without replacement has serious results.

Under normal circumstances the volume of water in the body is kept at a constant level and the amount of water lost is balanced by the amount taken in. In a temperate climate this is approximately 2.5 litres a day, while in hot climatic areas the amount is much higher and may reach as much as 5–8 litres.

EFFECTS OF WATER LOSS

If water is lost from your body amounting to 1–5 per cent of your weight (if you weigh 60 kg the amount would be from 0.6–3.5 kg), then the effects you experience are **thirst, discomfort, impatience** and various other effects which all add up to **loss of efficiency.** *The effects listed are those experienced when the water loss is within the lower limits.* Should you lose more water then, unless it is replaced, the results may be extremely serious. The following **water-loss chart** (based on the work of Dr E. F. Adolph, who studied the effects of water loss on men in the desert) shows the effects of increasing loss of water expressed as a percentage of your body weight.

The chart shows you how you will feel if you are not getting enough water, and it also shows you that **water** is your most important **survival requirement. You must have water to survive,** and at all times you must make every effort to satisfy this need. *Your need for water must ALWAYS take precedence over your need for food.*

PREVENT WATER LOSS

If your efficiency is to be maintained in a hot climate, your *daily* water requirement is not less than 5 litres, and in a cool climate (even a cold one) you need at least 2½ litres. If you are not getting these amounts (and these are **minimum** amounts) then you must do everything possible to conserve your body-water. The loss of body-water through perspiration can be very high if you are active in a hot climate and to cut down this loss, if little water is available, all your movements should be **slow, methodical** and totally **without rush**. You should also try to keep in the *shade* as much as possible and *keep your clothes on*, even adding some, if available, to conserve water-loss through perspiration.

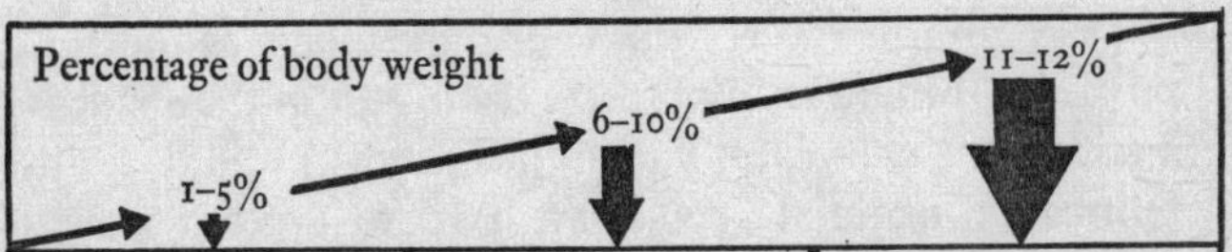

Percentage of body weight		
1–5%	6–10%	11–12%
Thirst	Headache	Delirium
Vague feeling of discomfort	Dizziness	Swollen tongue
Economy of movement	Dry mouth	Twitching
Impatience	Tingling in limbs	Deafness
No appetite	Blue tinge to skin	Dim vision
Flushed skin	Indistinct speech	Numb skin
Increase in pulse rate	Laboured breathing	Shrivelled skin
Nausea	Inability to walk	Inability to swallow
1–5% of body weight	6–10% of body weight	11–12% of body weight

Fig. 68 Effects of water loss from the body

Keeping your clothes on will mean you will be uncomfortable, but it will minimize evaporation of sweat.

In a cold climate, perspiration can also be a problem, and body-water may be lost through profuse sweating during heavy exercise unless care is taken with clothing – removing garments when necessary and replacing before chilling occurs (see also page 38). In very low temperatures, sweat may freeze, and this is another important reason for making sure that sweating is controlled.

METHODS OF KEEPING COOL

1. **Stay in shade** and restrict your movements as much as possible. If there is any breeze, try to rest in the shade in a position which places you in the breeze as well. Use any fabrics or materials you may have to erect a shelter against the sun.
2. **Travel only if absolutely necessary**, and restrict your travelling to very early morning, late afternoon or night.
3. **Wipe your face, brow, back of neck** with a cloth soaked in sea water, urine, after-shave lotion (passengers' luggage after an air crash will generally provide this – see page 187). Rub crushed succulent plants over the same areas. (Try rubbing the inside surface of a piece of freshly-cut cucumber skin on your brow to see how effective this is.)

NINE DO NOTS

There are very few 'Do Nots' in this book because it is a book of positive action, and negative thinking is best avoided in a survival situation. The **nine Do Nots** are all related to your requirement for water, and observing them will increase your survival chances. Read and re-read this Do Not list until it is fixed in your mind.

1. **Do not drink sea water** – whatever you may have read, or been told, or believe. Avoid even rinsing your mouth out with it, because the temptation to swallow 'just a little' may be too great – and the next amount you swallow may increase, and increase and increase! If you

do drink sea water, there is only one final result – death in a crazed delirium with your thirst a raging, unsatisfied demon!

Sea water can only rob your body of water; it can never supply it. *Sea water must never be drunk under any circumstances, whether diluted with fresh water, or undiluted.*

2. **Do not drink urine** – it has the same effect as drinking sea water – it makes your thirst worse.

3. **Do not drink gasoline, fuel oil, anti-freeze liquid, or alcohol.** When you have a raging thirst you may be tempted to drink liquids which, under normal circumstances, you would never think of drinking. If you drink any of these liquids instead of water, you will collapse and die.

4. **Do not drink water which tastes salty, soapy** or if obtained from a plant, is milky (unless you know it to be safe – i.e. coconut 'milk' is safe).

In some parts of the world, water from springs or soak-holes may contain high quantities of minerals which, in some circumstances, are extremely poisonous – and these may be the cause of a salty or soapy taste. If you come across water like this, treat it as though it is sea water and try and obtain fresh water from it, if possible using one of the methods set out below, such as Purifying Water by Condensation or Obtaining Water with a Solar Still. (See also Plant Water, page 146.)

5. **Do not drink any water on your first day of survival** (unless you are injured, or the supply of water is more than adequate). If your water supply is restricted, you should try to obtain at least 0.6 litre per day after your first day without any.

6. **Do not be afraid of drinking too much water.** Whenever you have the chance, drink all the water you can. You may feel saturated, but the feeling will soon

pass and the excess water in your body tissues will keep you going as long as possible under the conditions.

7. **Do not neglect your need for water in cold conditions.** It is easy to convince yourself that you only need a little water in a cold climate, but this is a mistake which must be avoided. Your intake of water must be kept at an adequate level. **Force yourself to drink water** under cold climatic conditions, even if you think you don't need it.

8. **Do not ration water if you only have a small amount.** If you are in a survival situation where your *total* available water is 1 litre or less – **Drink it all when you are thirsty**; it is quite useless to try and ration it.

9. **Do not eat any food if you are surviving in a hot climate and have less than 1 litre of water per day.** If 4 litres of water per day are available, then you can eat carbohydrate foodstuffs such as biscuits and sweets. Proteins (meat, fish, shellfish, cheese, beans, peas) use up a lot of water in digestion and so must not be eaten until completely adequate water supplies are available.

SOURCES OF WATER

Rain is an obvious source of water, but the lack of any method of collecting it means that a great deal will be wasted. A depression scraped in the ground will catch water, but if the earth is very dry or porous not much will be retained. Prevent it from running away by lining the depression with a waterproof coat, plastic sheet or large leaves.

If you are very short of water, let any spare clothing soak up any available water and wring the water into a container. In forest areas you can sometimes collect water from a sloping tree-trunk by twisting a piece of cloth (torn from clothing) around the trunk and leading the end down into any container you may have.

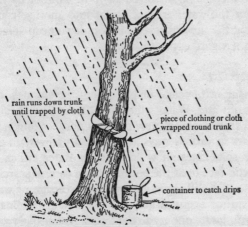

rain runs down trunk
until trapped by cloth

piece of clothing or cloth
wrapped round trunk

container to catch drips

Fig. 69 Collecting water during heavy rain

Dew is not so obvious as a source of drinking water, but in arid areas considerable amounts can form at night, particularly if the temperature difference between day and night is high. In some grasslands, dew is also common, and by dragging a piece of absorbent cloth (a cotton garment is suitable) through foliage, you may be able to collect enough water once you have wrung out the cloth, to satisfy your thirst.

Snow and ice should only be considered when you cannot obtain water in any other way. Changing snow and ice into water uses up valuable fuel, and particularly in the case of snow, a great amount of time is required. If you are able to melt snow in a container, you will find that melting a small amount first and then adding small amounts as more and more water forms will give you the best results. Ice is a better source of water than snow. Resist the temptation to suck snow or ice (if you have any other means of melting it) as it robs your body of heat, and the water gained this way is small. If water from melting snow or ice tastes 'flat' it is because there is no dissolved air in it. To remedy this you can pour the water from a height into another container, repeating the process several times; or you can aerate it by stirring it vigorously with a stick.

Ground Water

The diagram opposite shows places which may provide sources of water. Water which falls on the land as rain, or is derived from melting snow or ice is not lost, but normally reappears in various ways as it seeks a pathway to the sea.

Cliffs sometimes show seepages of water either on the actual cliff face or at the bottom, and a careful search along the base of a cliff sometimes yields a seepage of water, or even a spring. Seepages are generally slow at yielding water, but if you locate one try to dig a small basin-like receptacle for water to collect in. Isolated clumps of vegetation or patches of moss may indicate seepages along cliffs and these sites should be investigated.

Caves, particularly limestone caves which are formed by running water, sometimes contain pools or streams. Beware of going too far into caves, however, if you have no light and have no way of indicating your route.

Dry streams and *river-beds* look disappointing as sources of water, but quite often there is water not very far beneath the surface. Dig in any area which appears to be damp, or in the lowest part of the stream's or river's course. A good place to look is the outer portion of bends obviously followed by rivers or streams when they are flowing.

On sea coasts, water is often found *behind sand-dunes*, and digging down into the sand will sometimes give surprisingly large amounts of fresh water. (Take care when you taste it that it is fresh water, and not sea water.) When water is

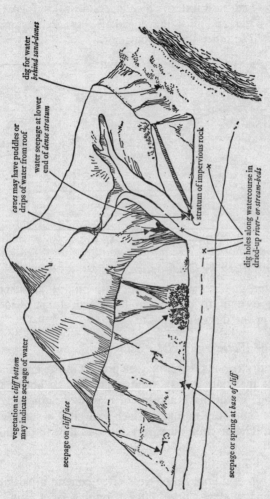

dig for water *behind sand-dunes*

caves may have puddles or drips of water from roof

water seepage at lower end of *dense stratum*

stratum of impervious rock

dig holes along watercourse in *dried-up river- or stream-beds*

vegetation at *cliff bottom* may indicate seepage of water

seepage on *cliff face*

seepage or spring at *base of cliff*

Fig. 70 *Where to look for water*

located in such places, both fresh *and* salt water may be present. The fresh water (which is less dense) will float on the salt water, and must be scooped off very carefully, using a sea-shell or other shallow container.

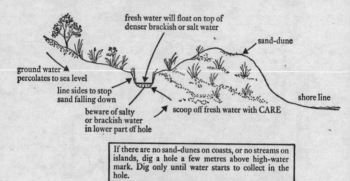

Fig. 71 Digging for water behind sand-dunes

Purifying Water by Condensation

Sea water, or water contaminated with mineral substances making it unfit to drink, can be effectively purified as shown in the diagram opposite.

Obtaining Water with a Solar Still

In very dry regions, water may be present in the ground or in plant material. It may seem impossible to obtain the water but if you have a piece of plastic sheeting a very effective 'still' can be made which will yield a surprising amount. The diagram on page 148 shows how to do this.

Plant Water

Vines, *roots* and *branches* of trees often contain a palatable fluid which is almost pure water. Climbing vines found in tropical forests yield a very large amount of this fluid, and it is an excellent thirst quencher, but the fluid **must be**

water vapour condenses on piece of cloth or clothing

hole scraped in ground, filled with sea water to be vaporized by hot stones

when cloth is saturated, wring it out into a container

Use sea water or water contaminated with minerals

push heated stones from fire into water with a large forked stick

heat stones in fire

Fig. 72 Purifying water by condensation

clear, not milky before it may be considered safe to drink. To get the fluid, cut lengths of vines, roots or branches and hold them vertically. It is important to make sure that lengths (about one metre) are actually cut off from the vines, or other plant materials – if you don't cut lengths, you

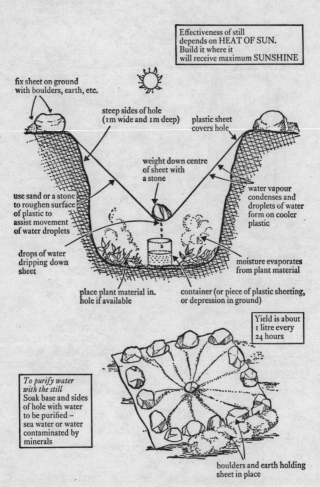

Effectiveness of still
depends on HEAT OF SUN.
Build it where it
will receive maximum SUNSHINE

fix sheet on ground
with boulders, earth, etc.

steep sides of hole
(1m wide and 1m deep)

plastic sheet
covers hole

weight down centre
of sheet with
a stone

water vapour
condenses and
droplets of water
form on cooler plastic

use sand or a stone
to roughen surface
of plastic to
assist movement
of water droplets

drops of water
dripping down
sheet

moisture evaporates
from plant material

place plant material in
hole if available

container (or piece of plastic sheeting,
or depression in ground)

Yield is about
1 litre every
24 hours

*To purify water
with the still*
Soak base and sides
of hole with water
to be purified –
sea water or water
contaminated by
minerals

boulders and earth holding
sheet in place

Fig. 73 Making a solar still using a plastic sheet

won't get any water. An airlock will effectively prevent any flow. (For the same reason, you punch two holes in a can of liquid – one for the liquid to escape and one for air to get in.)

If the fluid which flows when you cut the sections is milky, do not drink it – there is a strong possibility it will be poisonous and may also be a skin irritant. Leave such plants well alone.

Although climbing vines (leaves) will generally supply the most drinking water, the surface roots of trees may give you a reasonable supply. These roots will often be found near the surface of the ground, even in arid areas, and after exposing them should be cut into the lengths required.

If vines aren't present, and roots difficult to obtain, try branches of trees.

To drink from any of these water sources, hold your head back and lift the plant section vertically up above your mouth. The fluid will flow straight down into your mouth. Don't let the end of the cut vine, root or branch touch your mouth if you can help it – it may cause irritation.

SIGNS OF WATER

There are some species of animals, birds and insects which are never found far from water and, if you see any of these, then you can be sure that water is not too far away.

Animals

Although some mammals are able to obtain moisture from their food, the majority need water if they are to survive. If you should come across a well-worn animal trail where there are fresh 'signs', such as hoof-prints, browsed leaves, or droppings, then following it may lead you to water. (But look back at page 92 to make sure you don't get lost.)

Birds

All seed-eating birds need water. Flocks of finches seen feeding on the seeds of grasses or other plants are an excellent indication that water is not far away.

Pigeons, which feed on grain and seeds, will also be found near to a water supply, and generally, in the late afternoons, they move towards their water supply. Watch the flight of a pigeon, and if you see it flying straight and fast then it is highly likely that it is flying to its source of water. Pigeons drink a considerable amount of water, and *after* drinking their fill they fly slowly and carefully through the trees to their night roost. If you observe the flight *to* water or the return flight *from* it, you may be able to track down the source.

Insects

Some of the more highly organized insect communities require water and may lead you to their supply. Bees need water in considerable amounts, and wherever bees are to be seen you can be sure that water is within a reasonable distance, though the source of the water may be small. In tropical and sub-tropical areas, **mason bees** (the insects that build with mud) are a sure sign that water is very close, as they must collect the mud from a place which is permanently wet. Watch these insects' movements and if you can find their source of mud a little digging should expose a water supply. **Ants** are never far from water, and if you see a column entering and leaving a hollow in a tree-trunk, or a fallen log, there is a good chance that water is present. Test for water by inserting a 'dip-stick' into the hollow. If water is present, it may be extracted by tearing a piece of clothing, or by using a handkerchief, and forming the cloth into a ball on the end of a stick. Insert the ball of cloth into the water and draw it out when it is saturated. (If you have a survival kit with a rubber tube in it – page 15 – then it could be used to suck the water from such a hollow.)

> **Water is life
> Your survival depends on it!**

7. Food

Hunger, after your most immediate and pressing survival requirements have been satisfied, will indicate your need for food.

If conventional food supplies are not available you may ignore your hunger (without neglecting your need for water) for a day or so without any ill effects, but if you are to maintain your efficiency and strength you will need to satisfy your energy requirements – and this means you must eat!

In a survival situation there are two main categories into which possible foods and food supplies may be divided:

1. **Plant foods** – these are the *stationary foods* – those that don't run away.
2. **Flesh foods** – these are the *mobile foods* – those that have a tendency to run, fly or swim away, or can be classified as 'animal' in comparison to plants.

PLANT FOODS

There is an extremely good reason why the 'stationary foods', **plants**, are your most important food supply when you are in a survival situation – **availability**. Flesh foods may seem desirable, but they are not always easy to obtain, whereas there are hundreds of thousands of edible plants. This does not mean that you shouldn't make an effort to obtain meat which supplies the body with muscle-building proteins, but many plants also contain proteins together with carbohydrates which supply energy, and **you can** survive successfully on an exclusive plant diet without any flesh foods whatever.

In a survival situation you may have to eat foods which you would not normally consider suitable, but the nourishment of your body must take precedence over your tastes.

EDIBLE PARTS OF PLANTS

It is unusual to find a plant which is completely edible, and the majority have only one or two parts which you can eat. Depending on the particular plant, these are the parts which are edible:

Leaves, shoots, pith and bark
Roots, rootstalks, tubers and bulbs
Flowers, nectar and pollen
Fruits, berries, nuts and seeds
Gums and resins

THE EDIBILITY TEST

Before attempting to eat any plant, or any part of a plant with which you are not familiar, an **edibility test** must be applied. The edibility test requires **time** and **patience**, but the danger of eating poisonous material is very real and the test should be applied whenever you are not *completely* sure that what you are thinking of eating is safe. Always test one thing at a time, otherwise you won't know which food is affecting you.

1. Test the food *briefly* with your tongue to discover whether it has a disagreeable taste. Be very suspicious of anything which tastes very *bitter*, *acid*, or *like almonds*. If you do

detect such a taste, and some cooking facilities are available to you, then the food should be boiled in water for fifteen minutes, and then tasted again. If the disagreeable taste remains after this has been done reject the food. If cooking facilities are not available, soak the food in the running water of a stream for at least an hour. Test for disagreeable taste, and if necessary reject the food.

2. Take a *small* portion of the food and hold it in your mouth for five minutes. If no burning sensation appears after this time, swallow the food.

3. Wait for at least eight hours, and if no adverse effects appear (stomach pains, vomiting, nausea, diarrhoea) eat a small handful and wait a further eight hours.

If no ill effects appear after you have carried out the above tests, then you can safely eat the food.

SUMMARY

Plant edibility test
1. Taste briefly
2. Cook if possible
3. Hold small portion in mouth. If no bad taste – swallow
4. Wait eight hours. If no adverse effects – eat handful
5. Wait eight hours. If no ill effects – food is safe to eat

LEAVES, SHOOTS, PITH AND BARK

Leaves

The nutritional value of many leaves is quite high and, lacking any alternative, there is no reason why you should not obtain at least some of your energy requirements from many varieties of plants.

WARNING

Do not eat the leaves or any part of any tree, shrub or plant which has coloured sap. This is particularly important if the sap is milky.

You can safely make a meal of leaves if –
1. The sap or juice is not milky or coloured.
2. If you have applied the **taste test** and you cannot detect bitterness, acidity or a bitter almond taste.
3. You have applied, and they have passed the **edibility test**.

Grass

A group of plants whose leaves are an important food source are the **grasses**. The young leaves and shoots of all grasses are edible – some of them (**couch grass** is an example) have a sugar content which makes them pleasantly palatable.

Lichens

Lichens are distributed throughout the world in a wide range of habitats, and where no other food may be found you may find these plants growing on rocks or the trunks of trees. Scraped off trees or rocks, they may be eaten raw (despite their bitter taste) or boiled, which tends to reduce the bitterness. Lichens are a true emergency food and will sustain life when nothing else is available.

Seaweed

All seaweeds are edible. The reddish varieties are among the most palatable, although there is no reason why you should not eat any that are available. All seaweeds should be freshly gathered and eaten in moderation until the stomach becomes conditioned to the unaccustomed diet, otherwise they may cause diarrhoea.

Shoots

The leaves of many plants are too tough and fibrous to be utilized as food, even when cooked. The **shoots**, however, are often soft and succulent, and their food value sufficiently high to warrant the effort involved in collecting and preparing them.

Ferns

The young shoots of ferns ('fiddleheads') although edible *should not be used as food*. They have been used as survival or famine food for many years, but the recent discovery of properties in bracken shoots which are deleterious to human health (they have been found to be carcinogenic) makes it prudent to avoid all ferns as food.

Bamboo

If you are stranded in tropical areas the young shoots of bamboo provide a good source of food, and may be eaten raw or cooked. These shoots, which may be 30 cm or more in length, are most palatable if cooked. Before cooking, remove the outer sheath which is covered with fine hairs – these are a throat irritant and *must not* be eaten. Boil the shoots until tender and any taste of bitterness has disappeared.

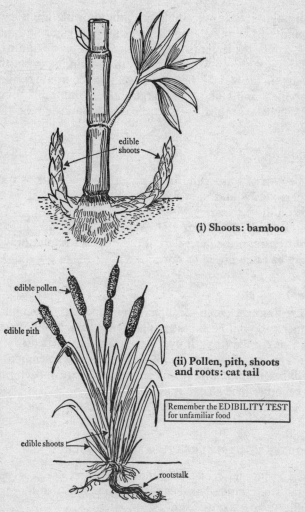

(i) Shoots: bamboo

edible pollen

edible pith

(ii) Pollen, pith, shoots and roots: cat tail

Remember the EDIBILITY TEST for unfamiliar food

edible shoots

rootstalk

Fig. 74 Plant food

Palms

All palm species are edible, and the growing leaf shoots
found in the middle of these plants are edible, raw or
cooked. In the larger palms (including the coconut palm –
see p. 163) the growing tip found in the top middle of the
trunk (in the region where the leaves join the trunk) is large,
succulent and edible. This large shoot is the 'cabbage' or
'Millionaire's Salad' – so called because removing this
growing tip destroys the tree.

Pith

The pith of some palm trees and tree ferns contains considerable amounts of starch, but cutting open the trunk to
obtain the pith can prove difficult.

The pith of the cat-tail (bulrush) is also a rich food
source, and if the outer part of the stem is stripped away it
may be eaten boiled or raw.

Bark

Strip away the outer bark of any tree and the green or white
inner bark will be exposed. This inner bark may be eaten
raw or cooked (toast it over hot coals), and particularly in
the spring will be found to be nutritious and sustaining.

Pines, birches, willows and all evergreens are worth trying
if no other food source is available.

– Remember to apply the edibility test.

ROOTS, ROOTSTALKS, TUBERS AND BULBS

The roots and rootstalks (underground stems) of plants
often store starch, but they may be so fibrous that they are
difficult to utilize as food.

Water Lilies

The roots and rootstalks of these plants store considerable amounts of starch and are very nutritious. In the temperate zones, water lilies' starch is in the rootstalks, and in the tropics in swollen tubers.

Although both rootstalks and tubers may be eaten raw, they are better boiled or baked by coating with mud or clay and placing in the embers of a fire. (See Fig. 75.)

Cat-tail (Elephant Grass)

The rootstalks are rich in starch and sugar, and may be eaten raw or cooked by boiling. If eaten raw the rootstalk may be chewed, or peeled and grated first into a kind of rough flour.

General Principles to Apply before Eating any Unknown Root, Rootstalk or Tuber

1. *Cook* by boiling, steaming or roasting for not less than 30 minutes.
2. *Taste* the food after you have cooked it.

The first of these two simple steps converts the raw starch into a digestible form, and the second tells you whether any *irritant* (in the form of calcium oxalate needles) or poison (in the form of Prussic acid) is present.

If calcium oxalate needles are present, you will experience a hot, stinging sensation on your tongue and lips. If Prussic acid is present, a bitter almond taste will be apparent.

If either of the effects is detected by your taste test – boil, steam or roast for a further 30 minutes then taste again. When the taste seems right apply the edibility test. It is better to be *hungry* and *sure* than *sick* and *sorry!*

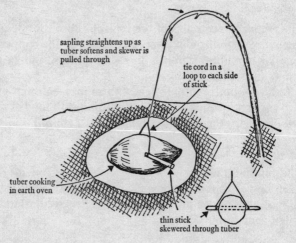

Fig. 75 Cooking 'indicator' for tubers steamed in an earth oven

FLOWERS, NECTAR AND POLLEN

Flowers

Not normally considered as food, the flowers and flower stalks of all **palms** may be eaten, if they are young and tender.

The flower heads of the **cat-tail** may be eaten raw, or cooked by boiling.

Nectar

Nectar is a concentrated carbohydrate which is found in large quantities in some varieties of flowers. It is not an important source of food, however, owing to the difficulty of collecting enough. If you should find flowers which yield nectar, break off the flower at its base, and suck the nectar out.

Pollen

The most important source of pollen as food is the **cat-tail** or bulrush, whose flower spikes produce large quantities. To collect the pollen, shake the mature flower heads or beat gently on a garment spread on the ground. Mix the pollen with water to form a thin gruel, or treat it as flour and mix into a stiff dough with water, then cook by steaming.

FRUITS, BERRIES, NUTS AND SEEDS

Fruits

It is important to have some simple rules to apply to the wide variety of wild fruits you are likely to encounter.

Rule *1*. Do not eat brightly coloured or red fruits unless you know them.

Rule *2*. Taste with the tip of your tongue, or bite off a very small piece of the fruit. **Spit out** immediately, and do not eat if there is any *bitterness, stinging sensation* or *nauseating flavour*.

Berries

Some berries contain dangerous poisons, particularly in the tropics. The nourishment you are likely to obtain from berries does not warrant experimenting with varieties which are unknown to you. Eat berries only when you are *completely sure* of your identification.

Nuts and Seeds

The same **taste test** applied to other parts of plants, such as leaves and fruits, should also be used with **nuts or seeds** which are not familiar to you. Tasting, in the case of nuts and seeds, may require actual chewing to release any substances which you may consider dangerous. You will not be harmed, however, if you do not swallow the chewed nuts or seeds, and you should simply spit them out if they are un-pleasant.

Nuts

The energy value of nuts is very high, and as a survival food they provide nourishment in a concentrated form.

The following nuts are all good food: –

Beech nuts. It is possible that beech nuts were one of the staple foods of our primitive ancestors. The kernels of beech nuts may be eaten raw.

Acorns. A mature oak tree produces an enormous number of acorns which are a valuable food source once the bitter tannin has been removed. Unfortunately, the removal of the tannin (which is not poisonous but makes the food in-digestible) is a long and tedious process. Dry the acorns in the sun and pound them into meal. Then put the meal into a shallow depression in sand or other material which will allow water to pass through. Water should then be poured on to the meal, and as it soaks down more should be added. After two or three hours of this leaching process, the acorn meal will be a dough-like mass. The dough may be diluted with water and boiled to make a type of soup, or it may be baked in hot ashes to make 'Indian Bread'. The Red Indians of America who made bread from acorn-meal dough first mixed it with red clay before baking it. If you wish to try this, shape the dough into a long 'sausage', divide it into twenty parts and then mix thoroughly into it some red clay corresponding in amount to one of the twenty parts. (Thus, the proportion of clay to dough is one part clay to twenty parts dough.) Cover the mixed dough with leaves and bury in the hot ashes of a fire for about 10–12 hours. Your bread should then be ready. It will be black in colour, but nutri-tious and sustaining. The red clay acts as a leavening agent (like yeast in 'true' bread).

Pine nuts. The cones of pine trees when heated will open, and with a little persuasive shaking release their nuts. These nuts are a high-energy food.

Other edible nuts which will provide you with sustaining food sources are:

Chestnuts, hazelnuts, walnuts, hickory, butternuts, peanuts, pecans, cashew nuts, almonds.

The Coconut

A very important food plant found throughout coastal tropical areas and the whole of the Central Pacific region is the coconut palm. These palms may be up to 20 metres high, with fronds 8–10 metres long. The coconuts are large and are covered with a thick husk which allows the nuts to float in the sea. The nuts are the principal food of the palm but the 'Millionaire's Salad' or 'cabbage' is found at the top of the palm itself, just above where the leaves and trunk join, and this is a good food also.

It is the nut, however, which provides a wide variety of food, and it is completely possible to survive indefinitely on coconuts and fish.

Edible Stages of the Nuts

The nuts pass through various stages from the time when they are fully formed on the palm to when they fall to the ground and germinate and form a new palm.

The young immature nut has a jelly-like lining which is good to eat, and at this stage is filled with cool delicious milk. To extract the milk from young or mature nuts, puncture two of the 'eyes' at the blunt end of the dehusked nut, using a thin, sharp stick or other thin implement – the milk may then be poured, or sucked, out.

The 'meat' of the nut is formed as the milk is absorbed, and if you shake a nut you can get a fairly good idea how

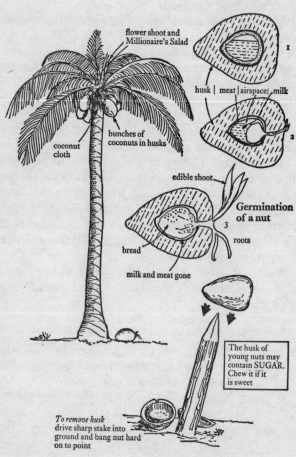

flower shoot and
Millionaire's Salad

1

husk | meat | airspace | milk

2

bunches of coconuts in husks

coconut
cloth

edible shoot

**Germination
of a nut**

3

roots

bread

milk and meat gone

The husk of
young nuts may
contain SUGAR.
Chew it if it
is sweet

To remove husk
drive sharp stake into
ground and bang nut hard
on to point

Fig. 76 Coconut palm and edible stages of the nut

much meat has formed from the sound of the milk sloshing about.

When the nut germinates as it lies on the ground, the meat and the milk are both used up and a spongy mass, known as the 'bread' is formed. The 'bread' is excellent food, and may be eaten raw or roasted. The sprouting leaves may also be eaten, and they supply vitamins – an obvious lack in most survival diets.

Extracting the mature nut from the rather tough husk can be difficult, but if a stout, sharpened stake is placed in the ground, as shown in the diagram, it can be used to prise off the husk. Alternatively, use your knife or hatchet to split the husk lengthwise into removable segments. The husk of very young immature nuts sometimes contains sugars, and chewing a piece will soon show whether any are present.

Once you have removed a nut from the husk it is not difficult to get at the meat – just tap the nut sharply on a stone to split it and scrape out the meat using the sharp edge of a shell, or knife.

Seeds

The safest and most reliable source of food from seeds is found throughout the world in the grasses – none are poisonous. All the cereals used by people the world over are grasses – millet, rice, oats, wheat, barley – and, although these named species are not always easy to find, it is comforting to know that any grass you find which has ripe seed heads may be used as food.

Important
Beware of **ergot poisoning**. If you should find **black grain-sized particles** on seed heads – discard them at once. They may be the fungus called **ergot**, which is *dangerously poisonous*.

To harvest grass seeds, cut a bundle of stalks with their seed heads, then beat them gently on bare rock, or on a garment so that you can collect the seeds together. Rub the seeds vigorously between the palms of your hands to husk the seeds, then winnow the seeds by tossing them gently up into the air, so that any breeze can blow away the husks while the seeds fall back to the ground.

Cooking

If absolutely necessary, grass seeds may be eaten raw, but if you have any means of cooking them they may be boiled or scorched on a heated stone. Doing either of these things makes the grains far more digestible.

GUMS AND RESINS

A minor source of food are the gums and resins. They are formed when sap from some trees seeps out through cracks in the bark and hardens on exposure to the air.

Plant gums are identifiable by their solubility in water, whereas the resins are insoluble. The resins found associated with all pine trees are edible and may be sometimes gathered in sufficient amounts to be utilized as food.

FLESH FOODS

Mention 'flesh foods' to a hungry man and he is likely to see a thick, juicy steak in front of him.

In a survival situation, however, there is likely to be a considerable difference between dreams and reality, and anything which walks, flies, swims, crawls, wriggles or just sits and grabs its food as it floats by is likely food for a hungry survivor. You may have to overcome a certain amount of prejudice before attempting unaccustomed foods, but it is always worth remembering that what may seem repugnant, even nauseating, to some people, may be almost a staple diet for others. Here for example is a recipe for 'Yam Pudding' as described by an Englishman who lived among the natives of the New Hebrides: 'Cook your yams, then mash them. Stuff animal titbits (eels, grubs, bits of birds, etc.) and edible leaves into the middle . . .' This was his daily diet for a year, and even after all that time he still liked yams!

GENERAL EDIBILITY RULES FOR FLESH FOODS OF ALL KINDS

1. The flesh of all mammals is safe to eat when fresh and unspoiled. (The offal or insides of all mammals is safe too, *except* the livers of seals and polar bears, which at some times of the year may be poisonous due to excessive quantities of vitamin A.)

2. The flesh of all birds is safe to eat – even sea birds and carrion eaters – although the flesh of these species may not be particularly palatable.

   All birds' eggs are edible when fresh, and they are also good food when they contain embryos.

3. The flesh of all lizards, snakes, frogs and salamanders is edible. Salamanders may have poisonous glands in their skin; they should be skinned before cooking and eating. *You will be perfectly safe if you skin all the species listed and eat only the flesh.* **Do not eat toads.**

4. The flesh of all fish is **not** safe to eat. The proportion of edible fishes to poisonous fishes is high, but it is important that you have some simple identification method which will enable you to decide whether any particular fish is safe or unsafe to eat.

Rule One

Do not eat any fish which is not fresh and does not feel and look right (it should not be soft, flabby, dull) **and does not smell right!**
It is particularly important in the tropics to follow this rule – fish which has putrefied (and this can occur in a very short time, even minutes, after the death of the fish) forms dangerous poisons and *must* be avoided.

Rule Two

Do not eat fish which lack scales. This rule should be applied to *all* fish which are completely unknown to you.

Rule Three

Do not eat any fish which does not look like a fish! Here are some examples:
You must avoid fish which are shaped like a box (**box fish**); inflate themselves like a balloon after being caught (**puffer, swell** or **blow fish** and the **porcupine fish**); looks like a pig with a snout-like mouth (**pig fish**); resembles a rough stone (**stonefish**) – this last fish is extremely venomous. It is found lying in shallow water in coral-reef areas. The spines on its back inflict serious wounds if you should stand on them.

Rule Four

Never eat any internal organs of fish – even fish which you know to have safely edible flesh. The liver in particular may be dangerously poisonous.

SHELLFISH

All shellfish have edible flesh and none are poisonous if they are fresh and have been gathered from an unpolluted area –

highly likely, if you are stranded on a coastline miles from civilization.

In tropical areas there are several species of shellfish which can inflict dangerous bites. These are the **cone shells**. They always live *under* cover (generally under blocks of coral), and great care must be taken when searching for shellfish on coral reefs that you do not inadvertently pick up one of these venomous shellfish.

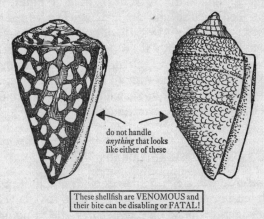

do not handle *anything* that looks like either of these

These shellfish are VENOMOUS and their bite can be disabling or FATAL!

Fig. 77 Cone shells

Shellfish are found in a variety of habitats ranging from sandy, tidal beaches, to rocky, exposed coasts and coral reefs. Some inland lakes and streams also contain shellfish, but it is important to remember that if they are gathered from such areas they may contain harmful parasites and should always be cooked before eating.

Bivalves, the shellfish with two hinged shells, are a good source of food and are often present in considerable numbers on sandy beaches. Some species may be found near, or even on, the surface of the sand, or they may be found at varying depths. Quite often you can locate them by

shuffling your bare feet through the water-saturated sand
between the high and low tide lines.

Some bivalves are found attached to rocks (mussels, rock-
oysters), and these species may generally be gathered at low
tide.

Shellfish with cone-shaped or spiral shells may occasionally be found as sand dwellers, but the majority live on or
near seaweed, or in rocky areas.

The large limpet-like **abalone, ormer or paua**, is an
excellent food shellfish, and although they live permanently
underwater are well worth gathering. When they are undisturbed they are slightly raised from the rocks on which
they live, but at the slightest alarm they clamp down tightly
and can only be dislodged with a knife. It is possible, with
care and stealth, however, to snatch these shellfish from the
rock before they become firmly attached.

LOBSTERS, CRAYFISH AND CRABS

All these creatures are rich sources of food. Lobsters and
crayfish must generally be trapped (see page 128), but crabs
can sometimes be found on rocky shores, sheltering under
rocks when the tide is out. In some parts of the world land
crabs and coconut crabs are also found, and they are
common on some islands in the Pacific.

OCTOPUS AND SQUID

Sometimes when fishing on rocky coasts you may catch an
octopus and the flesh is very good food if it is first beaten to
soften it, and then boiled. To kill an octopus, reach up
under the mantle which has an obvious pocket-like opening, seize the 'innards' of the animal and turn it 'inside-
out'. The tentacles are the part to use for food, and to

prepare them for cooking simply cut them off and hit against a rock.

Squid should be treated the same way, beating the flesh before cooking.

INSECTS AS FOOD

The thought of eating insects may seem strange to many people, but in many parts of the world they are a highly sought-after delicacy.

Locusts, when lightly roasted, are good food, but it is the larval (grub) stage of beetles which are generally the easiest to find (often in rotting logs) and which will yield considerable nourishment. The famous 'witchetty grubs' of the Australian Aborigines are beetle larvae, and any beetle larvae may be eaten by simply grasping the grub by the head and biting off the body. The flavour is not unpleasant, and is rather like peanut butter. If you prefer to eat these delicacies cooked, then they may be lightly roasted on a heated stone.

See preparation of flesh foods (page 180) for a more detailed list of survival foods.

HOW TO PRESERVE MEAT AND FISH

The capture of a large animal which yields an abundance of fresh meat, or the catching of more fish than you can comfortably eat in a short time, poses a food preservation problem.

The problem itself is simply stated – how should you go about treating a considerable quantity of fresh meat or fish in order that it will not spoil, and will remain good to eat?

The answer is almost as simple – **dry it**.

Drying food can be done by heating over a fire, or by leaving it in the sun. The use of sunshine is preferable since drying by fire may *cook* the food, whereas all that is required is the removal of moisture.

Drying of meat not only preserves it but considerably reduces its weight and volume. You can reduce 500 grammes of fresh meat to approximately 190 grammes by drying.

A Drying Method

One of the difficulties involved in drying meat and fish is to protect it from flies while the moisture is being removed, and the best way is to keep the meat or fish in a continuous cloud of smoke.

Make a simple, open framework on which strips of meat or fillets of fish may be laid, and maintain a smoky fire underneath this framework. The diagram shows you how to make such a drying frame. It should be constructed so that the fire is not too close to the open framework, as you do not want cooking heat. Do not add grass and leafy material to

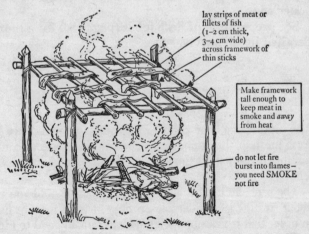

lay strips of meat or fillets of fish (1-2 cm thick, 3-4 cm wide) across framework of thin sticks

Make framework tall enough to keep meat in smoke and *away* from heat

do not let fire burst into flames — you need SMOKE not fire

Fig. 78 Drying meat on a smoke fire

the fire to make smoke as plant oils will be driven out and will settle on the food giving it a nasty taste. Depending on the weather, and the heat of the sun, the drying process may take two or three days and you will get the best results if the smoke is maintained all the time and the fire is never allowed to burst into flame.

Once it has been dried, the meat or fish will keep indefinitely. It may be chewed just as it is, or it may be broken up and boiled to make a stew or soup.

HOW TO PREPARE AND COOK FOOD

There are four principal methods of cooking, and even when you lack pots you can still use one of these methods so long as it is possible to light a fire. The four cooking methods are:

> Steaming
> Roasting
> Broiling
> Boiling

STEAMING

All foods can be cooked by steaming, and it is one of the most effective ways of softening many really tough, fibrous plant foods.

In many parts of the world 'earth ovens' have been used for hundreds of years to cook food, and you can easily use the same method. The earth oven is a foolproof method of cooking, provided some simple principles are followed.

To Make an Earth Oven

1. Dig a pit in earth or sand approximately half a metre deep, half a metre wide and one metre long.
2. Line the bottom of the pit with stones – smooth, water-

Stage I: Preparation of the oven

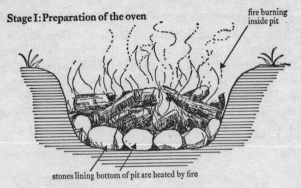

fire burning inside pit

stones lining bottom of pit are heated by fire

Stage II: Cooking the food

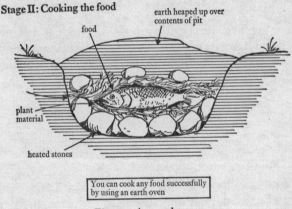

earth heaped up over contents of pit

food

plant material

heated stones

> You can cook any food successfully by using an earth oven

Fig. 79 An earth oven

worn stones are best, if they are available. Light a fire on top of the stones and stoke it up so that a considerable amount of heat is generated in order to heat the stones.

Extra stones should be added on top of the fire and they will sink down through it as the wood burns.

3. When the fire has burned to embers the stones will be heated. Remove any unburned fuel. The extra stones you have added should be pushed up the side of the pit with a

stout, forked stick, and placed on one side ready for use later.

4. Cover the heated stones in the bottom of the pit with a layer of green leaves about a handspan thick. Place the food to be cooked on the leaves, sprinkle with water, then cover over with a further layer of plant material. This second layer should be thick enough to prevent earth or sand from reaching the food.

5. Place any heated stones you have removed on top of the layer of leaves, then cover the pit contents with earth or sand and beat it down to seal in any steam.

Cooking Times with an Earth Oven

The following are approximate times for cooking of some representative foods in an earth oven. It does not matter if you leave any food longer than the times stated, because you cannot spoil food by overcooking in an earth oven since it is cooling continuously.

Food	Cooking Time
Meat on the bone such as a haunch of deer, goat, pig	Not less than 2 hours per kilo
Birds, such as duck, sea bird, woodhen	3 hours
Fish (medium) – unskinned	1 hour
Eel – unskinned	1 hour
Crayfish, lobster and crabs	1–2 hours
Cat-tail, palm leaf bases	1 hour
Cat-tail rootstalks and roots	3 hours
Fern 'fiddleheads'	1–1$\frac{1}{2}$ hours
Cat-tail pollen in cakes	2–3 hours
Acorn-meal dough	3–4 hours
Bark (inner)	6–8 hours
Seaweed	3–5 hours

ROASTING

Roasting does not require any equipment and there are various ways you can roast food, provided you have the one necessity – a fire.

The simplest method of roasting is to place food directly into the hot ashes which form the base of a fire. Protect the food by wrapping it in leaves or clay (see Preparation of Flesh Foods) and then bury it in the ashes which should be heaped up over the top of it. Provided the fire is not stoked up on top of it it may safely be left for several hours to cook.

Shellfish are one of the easiest foods to cook by roasting. You only need to pile them on to the embers of a fire and when the shells open they are ready to eat.

Roasting in a **stone oven** is an effective method you can use to cook food to perfection. The diagrams opposite show two methods of making such an oven.

The simple oven (Fig. 80 (ii)) is quickly made, but is intended for temporary use, compared with the type which can be built in a bank (Fig. 80 (i)). If you are likely to be camping in one place for a considerable period, and the materials are available, then this is the type of oven to make.

BROILING

Broiling is another name for barbecuing and it is a good method for cooking meats of all types.

Skewer the food on a sharp, green stick and then support it over a bed of very hot embers until it is cooked. Fig. 81 shows one method of doing this. Make the fire in a pit scraped in the ground, and when it burns down to embers support the skewered food over it as shown. Pieces of meat, crabs, and lobsters can be skewered and broiled in this fashion. Remember to turn the food occasionally.

Hand-held broilers or skewers may be used for con-

(i) A stone slab oven built in a bank

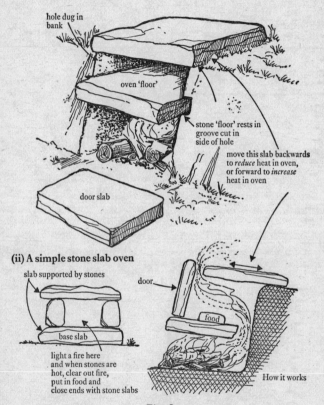

hole dug in bank

oven 'floor'

stone 'floor' rests in groove cut in side of hole

move this slab backwards to *reduce* heat in oven, or forward to *increase* heat in oven

door slab

(ii) A simple stone slab oven

slab supported by stones

door

food

base slab

light a fire here and when stones are hot, clear out fire, put in food and close ends with stone slabs

How it works

Fig. 80

trolled cooking. Various ways you can make such broilers from green plant stems are shown in Fig. 82. Fish is one food which is better cooked on a broiler of this type since it may easily soften and fall off into the fire if it is skewered on a stick.

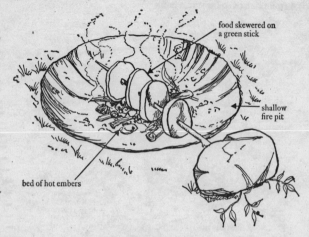

food skewered on
a green stick

shallow
fire pit

bed of hot embers

Fig. 81 Broiling or barbecuing

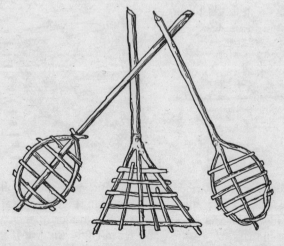

Fig. 82 Hand-held broilers made from green plant stems

BOILING

If you have an open metal container which holds liquid, boiling of water or food is no problem, but even if you have no container, you can still boil water if you have a piece of plastic, or a waterproof coat, or a large sheet of stout paper.

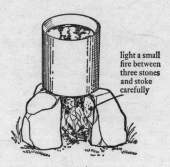

light a small fire between three stones and stoke carefully

Fig. 83 Supporting a container without a handle over a fire

First, light a fire and when it is burning fiercely drop into it two dozen or more stones about the size of hens' eggs. While these stones are heating, scrape a shallow depression in the ground and line it with the plastic sheet, waterproof coat or paper. Fill the lined depression with three or four litres of water. (This may require some ingenuity – you might need to use the plastic sheet to carry the water. Hold the corners in the form of a bag and carry the water to the depression. Then carefully lower it into the depression.)

When the stones are hot, lift them out of the fire with improvised fire tongs (two forked sticks with short, narrow forks are useful 'manipulators') and drop them into the water. Keep adding the heated stones from the fire and removing those that have cooled. In a very short time the water will be boiling and food to be cooked can be dropped into it.

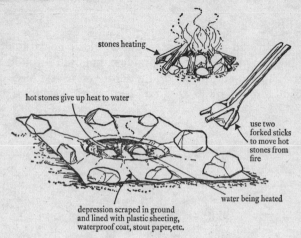

stones heating

hot stones give up heat to water

use two
forked sticks
to move hot
stones from
fire

water being heated

depression scraped in ground
and lined with plastic sheeting,
waterproof coat, stout paper, etc.

Fig. 84 Boiling water without a container

PREPARATION OF FLESH FOODS

SMALL MAMMALS

*Rabbit, Hare, Opossum, Marmot, Squirrel, Beaver,
Cat, Dog, Rat*

Small mammals like these should be skinned before cooking. Proceed as follows: lay the animal on its back, then cut across the skin from one hind-foot to the other, taking care not to cut open the abdomen. Sever the tail, then work the skin off like a glove. When you reach the forelegs, cut off the head and the feet, then pull the skin right off.

Gut the animal, cutting up along the abdomen and into the chest. Remove all the internal organs, including the heart and lungs. Take extra care when removing the liver that the gall bladder (a small sac filled with greenish-yellow fluid) is not ruptured. Also, if there are any whitish-coloured glands near the base of the tail (opossums and rats have these) be careful that you do not rupture them, releasing the sticky fluid they contain. (This fluid will contaminate the flesh, giving it an unpleasant taste, and should be thoroughly washed off if you have inadvertently cut these glands.) Wash the carcass thoroughly and cook by any of the methods described above.

Hedgehogs

It is not necessary to gut hedgehogs. Completely cover the hedgehog with a thick coating of clay and place in the fire. After cooking for approximately two hours, break open the clay ball and the spines will come away with the clay and the gut will be shrivelled, and of no consequence.

LARGE MAMMALS

Deer, Pig, Goat

Any large animal should be gutted as soon as possible after it has been killed. If you intend to skin the animal make sure you remove the skin *before* gutting, not after, otherwise you will find the job is extremely difficult.

Hindquarters should be removed by cutting in through the tissues until a joint is found. (Moving the leg will give an indication where the joint is.) Forequarters are easily cut off by severing the flesh between the shoulder-blade and the body.

On either side of the backbone, two long pieces of meat may be cut from any of the larger animals, and these 'back steaks' are particularly good for cutting into strips for drying. To remove these steaks from a carcass, cut along the side of the backbone with your knife held vertically, then cut once again horizontally, working your knife along so that the meat comes off in one long piece. Repeat on the other side of the backbone.

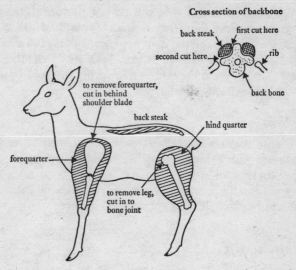

Fig. 85 Main cuts of meat taken from a larger animal, e.g. a deer

BIRDS

All types and sizes may be cooked, using the same method as that for the *Hedgehog*. Plucking and drawing is not necessary. Remove the head and feet, and plaster clay all over the body until the feathers are completely coated to a thickness of two or three centimetres.

FISH

Clean and cook fish as soon as possible after they are caught. This is particularly important in the tropics where fish spoil very quickly. Remove the gills – this will bleed the fish – then gut it.

Do not eat the internal organs of *any* fish.

Cook by any method, but really big fish are better steamed in an earth oven.

SHELLFISH

Seasnails and freshwater snails, limpets and all small shell-fish should be smashed with a stone and boiled to make a soup.

Bivalves

Shellfish such as **oysters, mussels, scallops, cockles,** may be eaten raw, but it is always preferable to cook them if possible. They may be steamed in an earth oven, or cooked by piling them into a heap on hot embers. They are ready to eat when the shells open.

Sea-cucumber (*Trepang* or *Bêche-de-Mer*)

Found in tropical and sub-tropical waters on reefs and rocky shorelines. When cut open, the animal yields five strips of edible muscle which can be eaten raw, boiled or broiled.

Sea-urchins (*Sea-eggs*)

There are various species of these animals, and the part eaten is the egg mass (roe) which is exposed when the body is cut open. The roe may be eaten just as it is or chopped up with seaweed to make a relish.

Avoid the **needle-urchin** found in tropical waters. This species is black or reddish in colour and has brittle spines up to half a metre in length.

Sea-anemones

These animals make a good soup if simmered gently in fresh water. Wash them thoroughly to remove dirt and slime before cooking.

Abalone, Ormer or Paua

The muscular 'foot' and the stomach (which will generally be full of plankton) of this univalve are both edible and are excellent food. To remove the animal from its shell hook your finger under one end of the foot and tear it out of the shell.

The stomach will be found lying towards one end of the foot and is generally about the size of a small hen's egg in the mature animal. Eat it raw or roast it on a heated stone.

The muscular foot is too fibrous and tough to eat without treatment. Beat it hard between two stones, or hit it with a piece of wood while it is lying on a stone. After a few strong blows the meat will soften and may be boiled or roasted.

Octopus or Squid

The tentacles are good food after they have been 'tenderized' by beating with a stone or piece of wood. Cook by roasting or steaming in an earth oven.

Crayfish, Lobster, Crab

These creatures may be boiled, broiled or steamed. Crayfish and lobsters are excellent steamed, while crabs may be conveniently cooked by threading on a stick and broiling.

Snakes, Lizards, Frogs

Snakes, lizards and frogs should be skinned and gutted before cooking. Only the hind legs of frogs and the hind legs and tail of lizards contain enough meat to make their cooking worth-while. The whole of a snake's body (minus the head) yields a tasty, white meat, which tastes like salty chicken. Cook by steaming or roasting.

Turtles and Turtle Eggs

Along sandy, tropical shores, parallel tracks leading from the sea up the beach then back to the sea may indicate that a turtle has come ashore to lay its eggs. Follow the tracks to where there appears to be some major disturbance of the sand and by digging down you may reveal a considerable number of eggs. Cook by roasting (see *Eggs*, below).

A *turtle*, if seen out of water on a beach, should be turned on its back – *avoid being bitten or scratched while doing so* – and then killed by hitting it on the head with a heavy stone or club. Gut the turtle and reject all the offal, eating only the meat.

INSECTS

A minor source of food, but nevertheless abundant enough at times to provide a substantial meal.

Beetle Larvae and Termites

Eat raw or roast on heated stones. Do not overcook, otherwise all their nourishment will be lost.

Grasshoppers, Locusts, Cicadas

Remove wings and roast on heated stones.

EGGS

Fresh eggs (a fresh egg has no smell) may be boiled, steamed, roasted or eaten raw. To roast an egg, puncture the shell at the narrowest end with a sharp twig, then stand it upright in the hot ashes near the edge of a fire.

Eggs containing embryo chicks may be boiled or roasted, or the embryo may be removed and boiled with plant foods to make soup.

8. To Stay or Not to Stay – and What to Do if You Go!

If you are the sole survivor of a **plane crash**, or a **stranded vehicle**, there is a question which must be considered with great care: 'Should I stay with the wrecked aircraft or vehicle, or should I try to find my way back to civilization?'

There can be no hard and fast answer to this question, but it is possible to list the pros and cons which will enable you to make a decision –

REASONS FOR STAYING

1. An aircraft or vehicle which is known to be overdue will be the object of a search. Searchers, particularly if a search is being made from the air, will be looking in the first instance for the missing aircraft or vehicle, not the occupants – they come later.
2. An aircraft or vehicle is a much larger object than a person and is seen much more easily than a single survivor on foot.
3. A plane wreck or broken-down vehicle provides shelter against heat (through the shade it provides) and against rain and moderate cold. (The fuselage of an aircraft is not an efficient shelter against extreme cold.)
4. Materials for making **distress signals** are more readily available from a wrecked aircraft or vehicle (**oil, rubber,**

plastics for smoke-making, **headlights, horn** for light or sound signalling).

5. A crashed aircraft, particularly a large passenger aircraft, will almost certainly be carrying a considerable amount of food and water. First-aid materials and blankets will also be carried, and passengers' luggage will yield many survival aids.

6. Weather conditions, or the terrain, make travelling so difficult or dangerous that it should only be undertaken when there is no chance of a rescue party arriving.

REASONS FOR NOT STAYING

1. No sign of searchers have been heard or seen after a period of seven days.

2. No one knows that you are in a particular area, and there is no possibility that you will be missed for a very long period.

3. The position where you are stranded makes observation and discovery of the aircraft or vehicle from the air extremely unlikely, e.g. in dense forest.

4. To stay with the wrecked aircraft or disabled vehicle is more dangerous than leaving it. To be stranded at a very high altitude on a mountainside, or in a precarious position would be such a situation.

5. Search aircraft or searchers have been seen, but have not responded to distress signals, and several days have elapsed since they were seen.

Use this for-and-against list to make your decision to stay or go. If your decision is 'to go' leave a clear message which is easily seen. Give your name, the date (if you know it), what supplies you are taking with you, and the direction you are heading (this very important piece of information should also be marked on the ground with an arrow).

> And don't forget this manual!

Index